AMDEN BOG

AMDEN BOG

A NOVEL IN STORIES

DAVID ROSE

A special thank you to Devin, who knows the swamp, to Mac, who enjoys it, Ryan, who doesn't, and to Jill, lovers of the same inkwell are we.

Contents

MATINA'S TALE

When Tiama, Governess of Orisulan colonies, demanded jungle tour, a monkey climbed a branch and showed her his balls. After a time the monkey left and the Governess was fanned back from her fainting. The Governess, whose white skins would be eaten alive by the jungles and swamps, asked Rattat, Father of the Tour, if such place always held such surprise. And Rattat, Father of the Tour, say: You want jungle, bitch—be ready for surprise!

—Pelat proverb

When I was a little girl, Mama told me to stop watchin' people. It weren't that I made 'em uneasy, no, just that most folks never knew I was there. From our cabin I'd take my canoe and by nightfall had followed boatmen, croc hunters, and families bustlin' about in Amden proper. Mama, who'd plunk me in the bath as soon as tell me again how she worried I'd been abducted by no-goods, loved me even more than our solitude. And that's sayin' somethin', for it was an ardent one. Cast back in the willows and boa-vine, our lonely home sat sturdy on stilts that not even summer storms could buckle.

I once felt my watchin' people would end up makin' me a writer. Mama was a good reader, though she didn't care for it much. The books she did have I ate up, and after much naggin' she went into town to topple a new stack on our floorboards. It was in these leatherbounds where I saw their makers had picked an' plucked from the human way, big and small. With Mama's help I became about as well spoke as a swamp child with no last name ever could be.

Town was not somethin' Mama subjected herself to. The swarm of Pelats did not sit well with her at all. "Stay away from 'em, you hear," she'd say while shuckin' Apraz, gettin' the bundles ready for the tradin' docks. "They're not like us." I gotta say, though, I didn't really believe Mama hated them Pelats much— more just her way than anything.

If you're from Amden Bog, then you know all the beasts and critters we got lurkin' about. From a book, I recall our droopin', bright blue dragonfly is called the Bobilulla. Aside from those, the only nice creatures here are the magic frogs and the skittish deer. Everythin' else seems out to get you, and that's exactly what Mama said happened to my daddy when I was a baby.

If I had gone to school with the other kids, I would've just heard 'em say, "There goes the girl whose daddy was eaten by a swamp monster." Not all that big a fuss in these parts. Plenty of bog children grow up with kin in the bellies of crocodiles. But of course, Mama had to outdo herself and say it was no croc, but some rarer, fouler, meaner beast. I must give it to her, she stuck to her story, even when I realized she was just tryin' to protect me, perhaps herself a little too. No, my daddy ran away, leaving us girls to fend for ourselves.

My name is Matina. In some of my favorite stories, warriors and witches had lone, strong-as-all names. But in the bog, two-thirds a family with no last name only earned gawks and murmurs. Also, my parents being *Morth* and *Mortha* didn't help none. Rumors of inbreedin' bounced back even to my ears with as much earnest an' regularity as Mama's monster-ate-daddy story. I reckon it was all the gossipin' that drove her deeper into reclusive ways, draggin' me along kickin' and screamin' whenever I stepped too close to a dance or fireside puppet show in town.

And boy, Amden does have a town! Though "Amden" refers to every hut an' cabin specklin' our marshland, near the center rests an island large enough to house a thick nest of docks and buildings that've all grown or moldered into each other.

The town called to me, even its most rundown part that toppled into a graveyard busy slippin' back into the swamp. My books called such places a "necropolis," but that implied a city of all dead folks. The shanties leanin' against those tall point graves and the drunken no-goods lyin' about the tombstones gave the graveyard a mixed population.

From my earliest days, I loved our town. Yet festivals and even mischief require gettin' on with others, somethin' I was forbidden to do.

I had to take a different strategy. To develop my stories, I'd hurt myself. Yeah—I ain't tryin' to sound this and that, or gouge out some sympathy. It was diggin' into the mind of whomever was sufferin' on my parchment what demanded it. But even if Mama hadn't had a soggy sandal on my neck, I'd go scurryin' off if I ever found myself talkin' to folks any longer than a speck.

So I took to watchin' others, and cuttin' myself. Cuttin' started as a way to understand pains I didn't think I knew, but in time it didn't hurt so much at all, call it a pleasure even. Then the little slices gave way to bigger, better joys. Stealin' beer from the dock-men was one thing, but the day I discovered the zap of those magic frogs, my two habits Mama hated most fused together with a fury.

"You will *not* be sneakin' out of this cabin," Mama said, lickin' her lips as she sometimes did. "And those glow-belly frogs?! What's the matter? You incogitant? Gods cursed a lovin' mother." She inflated herself and talked like a man. "Gonna chomp on this little morsel—one of them swamp monsters will say one day—chomp on this one *gooood*."

Mama was funny when she wasn't tryin' to stunt my ambitions, but for all my ways that concerned her, the way she sometimes talked left me scratchin' my head. Usin' words like *sterling* and *incogitant* made it seem, the times Mama forced herself into town, that not only had she emerged from the willows but from the pages of history.

I once tried such words myself, and town folk I'd bump into told me such hadn't been muttered around here for a hundred years. It was like she'd come from someplace else, or had lived longer than other folks.

Odd-talker or not, she dragged me to a frog addict, missin' both legs from being bitten by some beast in the dark. Meanin' to scare me. I snuck back out to see that legless wharf rat. After bein' offered a barter I would accept many more times with many more men, I traded a few painful thrusts for a map to the best frog-giggin' hole.

I was like the character Cassada, the girl who sought life's riddles in purple dresses. Just drape me in one stitched in hides, rub some dirt on my arms, and into the swamp's night Cassada went. I hid the map like another scar. Followin' it, I'd gig glowers and squeeze 'em without mercy. In bliss, I'd imagine findin' a monster and interrogatin' it about a man called Morth.

Before fadin' entirely, for a time the idea affixed to me. A little courage got me talkin' to Rehtons, all of whom pointed me to our town's shaman. Boraor Rehton was apparently the local authority in animal lore, though I could never catch him at that rich-folks' cabin of his.

)(

Aside from never knowin' my dad, cuttin', and enjoyin' good times like beer an' frogs, there's another thing about me that may concern a well-wisher. Mama always told me to remember how lucky I am. My bones all worked and my auburn hair was pretty, and there were little boglings with no one in all Mulgara to tuck 'em in at night. I do try to remember this, and most times I do a good job, but it's also just as true that I suffer from a weird flu.

Every summer, just as the rains come billowin' in, I fall asleep and can't be woken until fall is at the door. I know this because tellin' me so is Mama, forcin' spoons in my mouth while I sleep the summer away.

I know this another way, though. I'll remember goin' to bed one night, right before the Party of the Rains—a celebration I'll attend someday, come the death of me—and then I'll come to, months later, rememberin' nothin' but the oddest of dreams:

I'm in the bathtub. To avoid Mama washin' my hair again, I sink below. But when I do, I sink too far and all the walls of the tub are gone. Kickin' soft and stretchin' forward like a frog, I swim through wet and welcomin' darkness.

Mama has rattled off a whole list of illnesses that must've combined to rob my memory in chunks. Mama remained stern it's a blessin', but my flu robs my memory good, even the memory of the flu itself. And Mama must have fed and washed me as diligent as a princess's servant. Come fall, I'd be sneakin' out again and would be back in the bog, healthy as if I'd merely suffered a good night's rest.

Bog—"wet ground"—isn't really doin' much justice to where we all live. It's a vast jungly wetland, scarred by deep channels and little lakes reflectin' the burnin' sun or the whiteness of the moon. Homes dot it, lit by night like scowlin' heads with square, orange eyes, or one blinkin', or a whole bundle of 'em roarin' out the reds and yellows of their fires.

It would have made Mama at least somewhat proud I obeyed her and avoided hoppin' up onto the road. It led due north from our town's most northern dock and ended up in Oxghorde.

Instead, my explorations were in the waterways and under the canopy, alone in my canoe, hummin' out the last feel-goods of a frog zap. But considerin' what came with all the nighttime adventures, I was likely just as safe on that road to Oxghorde, or in one of that big city's alleys I'd once read about.

Bugs and snakes were far from the only stirrers in the night. I'd been shot at by crossbows, heard and *felt* slung rocks crackin' against cypress.

The worst of it, around the time I outgrew my hide-skin dress and my breasts swelled to match Mama's, on a grassy island no bigger than a granddaddy croc I was pummeled by a shadow smellin' like liquor. I fought the man off for the most part. It was akin to the map-givin' wharf rat, just horrid and forceful. What his loins didn't, a few fingers did, and I suppose that makes the encounter a *coulda been worse.*

My knee to his groin allowed my paddle to his head. When I pushed off, sobbin' so loud I couldn't hear a bug, I took his canoe with me. It would've been a wonderful gift for Mama—would've sold somethin' nice. But I figured no explanation would make much sense, especially with my eye swellin'. So I sunk it somewhere deep and cut my swollen eye to let out the blood. Both felt good.

Before too long, my frog hole was empty. I'd gigged 'em all, though I suspect others caught on too. When I tossed the map, I did so with an idea. I'd just turned eighteen. Even if spyin' from a distance, I decided to risk a few run-ins with night-movin' men and go frog huntin' deep in the bog. Deeper than ever. The places where lanterns swung low.

Mama got me in those far-off fens, but in all fairness, it was only because, like her window locks, her warnins only encouraged me. "That koot's cabin," she'd said when I'd mentioned a hermit named Pauthor after I overheard some late-night frog hunters gabblin' on. "Stay clear of 'im, you hear? Not all of us who keep to ourselves keep to ourselves for sterlin' reasons." Pauthor, this painter, lived on the other side of the bog, clear across and over the town, near deeper waters, where strange plants grew and I hardly knew my way.

The first night that I was able to weasel out of my loose-locked shutters, I was back out and under the moon. If this hermit was a no-good, he was a special one. In Mama's eyes, I had seen, for once, that she actually meant it: her dislike for someone. Goin' to snoop for myself was the only thing I could do.

Doin' so led me to a swarm of frog addicts so numerous, in no time I was all but distracted: farmers on leaky rafts, Pelats with fastened cowhides stretched taut over logs, and croc hunters who cut through marsh like an axe head. I guess my whirlin' adventures out there were a lot like Cassada's, just hers were all given to her it seemed. I had to go out lookin' for mine.

I learned not to approach anyone by canoe. Stowin' it then pushin' out on a floatin' log worked best. Stretched out on my belly, paddlin' with my hands, I'd wade up to these other giggers. Catch 'em after they'd caught a frog or two—you could dance the night away on their rafts. I even stole a bushel of plucked Apraz once. Next day, I added it to Mama's baskets, hopin' to make her happier than a bog lark in spring. She studied 'em too, their sought-after middle, like a purple ear of corn wrapped in ball-moss husk with fuzzy tendrils burstin' out from the pups. My contribution, I do believe, went unnoticed. Fine by me. Less questions. Around that time, however, I'd start to shake if I remained frogless for a week or so. *That* was a bit harder to keep hidden.

X

Right before the Party of the Rains, Mama said that bit about Pauthor—all those things about not goin' over there and all those things that made me gear up to do it. And then, right on time, I woke up one night in my bed to learn summer'd just ended.

I knew this from the cookery and spoons an' changin' rags Mama'd displayed all about me. While I was chewin' on why I had to have such rotten luck, after a bit I noticed that I was alone. At first thinkin' this was an extension of my dreams, I pinched myself. Mama was gone.

I'd ripened into womanhood, somethin' not lost on the dock-men givin' me a stash of coins under my preferred floorboard. Girls my age were runnin' off and marryin', and I s'posed I'd run into some fishermen one night who wasn't too ugly a face. But for the time being Mama still had an iron grip on me, least she tried, and her absence puzzled me somethin' fierce.

Gettin' back on my feet helped some. I could ponder all night why Mama had left me to my lonesome, but I also knew such pon-derin' was a waste of a perfectly good night. My first night awake in a good long while, and there was a place I wanted to go. I stowed my concerns for the time bein' and scooted off in my canoe.

When I got there, for a few moments I refused to breathe. I'd weaved between froggers, avoiding my own cravin', and made it to the other side of the bog. Now facin' Pauthor's cabin, his torches flickered and gleamed off the deep channel out his front door. Cows made their cow noises in the distance, as did their accom-panyin' Pelats, but my eyes were affixed on the hermit's window.

Stowin' my canoe in a reed bed, I tiptoed through muck. I wanted to see this codger. I figured it was a good night's work for just comin' out of my flu coma. Before long, the window's curtain showed itself to be two, drawn to the middle. In the open sliver between 'em was grey hair matted on top of a downward face. Near me, Rigl heads rose in the outer gloom. I felt his torches' heat. Then I fell into a hole.

Scramblin' to my feet, I saw I was in the maple-leaf web of what first appeared to be the pushed-down paw print of a giant croc. But as my eyes keened, I saw it had a fifth claw that went sideways like a thumb. Crocs don't have thumbs.

All of Mama's stories, and here was a print of some beast big enough finally to put Morth in a belly. For all the contradictions I'd heard—*his boat capsized, he went deer huntin', your daddy went swimmin' after dark like a plum fool*—all Mama had to do was skip the wharf rat and find me one of these prints in the mud.

My mind swirled, then eventually she steadied.

I knew the score.

Mama's slip-ups and this hermit's reputation all came together like flotsam on a log.

It was right out of the *Soliard Tales*: An old recluse up in amethyst hills made pastries for all the good children in the neighborin' dale. To scare off the bad children from sneakin' up there and stealin' all the goodness for themselves, he spent a whole year carvin' two big and perfect feet. When Pothux, the Bully Who Never Shared His Toys, journeyed up there with his toadies, they only found the deep footprints of a lumberin' giant.

My eyes kept bouncin' from the paw print to the hermit's silhouette in the window. I'd always wondered what kind of yellow-belly my daddy was for leavin'. If I ever met 'im, I'd put a knee to him first, then a hug second, maybe. Even if I was a girl who didn't go to birthdays and dances, books shined bright the truth how daddies and daughters were s'posed to act. But if this print really weren't from no croc—

)(

Funny how a noise can do it. Inside the cabin, a jar or somethin' busted. All the screams and tantrums that came after it shook me back to my wits. I solved this little riddle, not a riddle at all once weighin' a thing or two about who was involved.

Mama had told this Pauthor to make this print. I'd pulled the wool over her eyes more times than I could count on a hundred feet, but she had her tricks too. Knowin' I'd never listen, and knowin' this man's not needin' some girl nosin' around in his affairs, they made an accord and the art man had put down his brushes long enough to stamp out a phony print that had stopped me good. I chuckled about it all as I headed back to my canoe.

A Bobilulla burst to life above me, scarin' me half out my leggings. They hover over you if you stand still and are pleasant. I did. I was.

I saw all the other paw prints.

I didn't know them to be that at first, of course. There were a lot of pools in these parts. And that's what I took 'em for. But the Bobilulla's dazzlin' blue went right over the deep tracks of a movin' beast, and a slide from a draggin' belly as wide as the world. Whatever had made all these marks had done so recent, too recent, within minutes perhaps...and slipped back into the water right past my toothpick of a canoe.

Another Bobi', this time if tied to a string like a blazin' kite, would've been helpful when I started creepin' toward the hinterland where the tracks had come out of. But once the hermit's torchlight was behind me and my eyes adjusted, I made my way to a spot with no Rigl and few trees. The stars were bright enough here I could've walked unbothered while reading a book.

I saw globs and gut, flung or smeared into the slide. I neared a toppled fence, or what could be mistaken for one.

At the time I hadn't smelled cow shit before. Fondlin' a splintered end of this fence, my nose picked up the thick, dumbfoundin' stench of the cows and the sweet copperish waft of what had to be one of 'em's blood. I was busy lookin' down at the rail I'd stepped over when a voice said, "You bout the last ting I spek to see tonight."

It took a few more words to ring in my ears I wasn't face to face with a brainless swamp varmint, but my first ever Pelat. "Don't mean to intrude," I managed to say, fightin' off a stutter that came from half nerves and the other half my grinnin'. "You missin' a cow?"

"Oh yes yes," he said, flingin' up his arms, one of 'em revealin' a wooden club. "Yes, missing many cow."

What a leathery monkey of a man. Tattoos shrunk and expanded as he bustled about, cussin' in his tongue and puffin' a pipe. When I offered to help him hoist a few fence rails from the trampled mud, I tell ya, the look he gave. I finally asked, "What it look like?"

But the little man was already gone. He cursed me, he cursed his neighbor, he cursed what I heard as "big lizards" before disappearin' into the rest of his herd.

"Why not build a better fence?" I hollered. "The big lizards! Comin' all the time to eat yerr cows."

Pauthor had to have heard this. The gods only knew what he'd come roarin' out of his cabin to do to a trespasser.

Runnin' back to my canoe, I heard the Pelat, "Day only come summer time."

)(

For a moment last night, I'd pictured the interrogations. That Pauthor first—maybe spread my legs for 'im if it got him talkin'. Mama next, scarin' the cranes from the trees with how loud I'd be yellin': "Enough is enough!" Lies take more lies, as they say.

Puffin' up to people, though, wasn't really my way, and my startlin' discovery had brought me back to scour over my books. I couldn't find the collection of drawins I'd swore I'd seen once: mythical beasts from the Other Lands. I tossed the final book and walked right past my returnin' mother. Kinda strange, but I wasn't really in the mood to talk, especially when she started in on the *where ya goin*s. I figured I'd explain all soon, and that now I knew she was tellin' the truth all along. I was on my way to try an' find our town's shaman again.

The bog's lastin' hum had always elevated him, and the first time I'd asked for directions to his home, that elevation only got higher. About Boraor Rehton were stories of taming killer craw-fish, escortin' lines of crocs to waitin' tanners, and just about every tale to help fishermen set trotlines or a grown-desperate frogger find new ways to ensure a few more zaps. On the other side of a wall of willow, I once again was at the foot of his grand and dark-wood home. At the door stood two spear-wieldin' guards, both clad in croc hides and bronze armor.

When they eventually marched off to occupy someplace else, I shimmied through the nearest window. The room I fell in held more books than I could read in two lifetimes. Joinin' 'em along the walls were heads of animals, all lookin' a bit smarter than the whole animals that were posin' down on the floor. Cauldrons, gurglin' vials—all this, but no people, 'cept me. A nailed-up scroll had some paw prints inked all over it.

"Shaman Rehton, I—"

Though I'd froze, my eyes still scanned the scroll. It wasn't just to appear calm, as an invited guest may, but also because I'd found sure drawins of the prints I'd seen last night.

Pullin' my eyes from the parchment to glance who'd caught me, my glance became a stare. Her hair was short as a boy's. Though she was clear across the room, the sparklin' ornament about her neck shined as pretty as 'er face.

"Shaman is gone," I said. "And I'm right behind 'im."

She walked toward me, crinklin' her forehead. "And you are?"

I wasn't no thief, not today anyhow, and my wants were as understandable as any bookworm. I pointed to the scroll. "I saw some of these in the mud."

Between the Pelat and now her, I didn't know if whatever was makin' these prints was somethin' others knew about or what. Though a full hand shorter, she bullied me aside to study the scroll. Doing so, I found myself studyin' how she'd rubbed up against me.

"Ansul's ass," she said, then took 'er eyes off the scroll to grab off the shaman's wall some tambourine-lookin' thing. The way she fiddled with it, all important-like, made me stare at it too.

"What's that?" I asked.

"A balial. They are used to…" but then she stopped. Turnin' to me with eyes sparklin' like that necklace, "Where did *you* see those prints?"

This bitch's tone made it clear, I'd shed the tail of a burglar and popped out the four slimy legs of a mud-stackin' peasant. "In parts rich girls don't go."

"Take me there?"

"Why not," I said, remindin' myself for some reason of the Pelat. "What is it anyhow?"

She unwrapped a band around her wrist.

On the scroll we'd been gawkin' at, names of animals were written under all the prints. The *Gorsuka* was what we both were interested in, and under her band, she had a tattoo of a Gorsuka print that matched the one on the shaman's scroll—and the one I'd seen in the mud.

Even I knew there were at least two cults lurkin' about Amden. One remained hidden 'cause our land's wide outlawin' of all things black magic. But no hangin' or impalin' stopped these demented folks, almost always from Pelliul and Oxghorde, comin' to our graveyard and tryin' to summon up some ghost. I could still recite Mama, tryin' as always to scare me: *Only one soul black ever kept its composure so,* and *this spirit so sinister, the simple hells that themselves once hunted him did bid a tidy retreat.*

Mama sure could tell 'em, and so could this girl.

She informed me she was one of the shaman's pupils. Her animal tattoos reminded me of the second cult. I'd seen 'em on some nights and figured 'em for frog-giggers. Instead, the cult brightenin' our cypress with their torches were the beast worshippers.

"Ever seen one?" I asked. "A Gor-whatever?"

"They're only here in the summer," she said. "But I saw one's tail once—well, quite sure I did. Nobody knows where they come from." Beating me to my own question: "Even Shaman Rehton, but we are working on that. Those majestic beasts are life's mystery and beauty wrapped in one."

I couldn't help but compare this airy pupil's poetry to what was left of that Pelat's cow, or his fence for that matter.

She startled me good by askin', "So are you snooping around because you want to be in that animal cult?"

"Why? I look the lost soul?"

I thought an hour'd passed before she said, "No, not at all. No, just—if so, you're in the wrong office, sweetheart. It's all potions and charts and memorizing ludicrous names here." She startled me even better by grabbin' my ragged flounce. "You've seen more swamp than most. Haven't you, sweetheart?" I was confused but not upset by the nickname, a little excited too, and both swelled when her hand went from my flounce to my hip.

"Your body is so firm," she said.

"I tear off Apraz."

"Squirrely men all over our bog walk on flimsy branches for that silly vegetable. Your arms feel…more like a fisherman's. I bet I know—your family harvests Rigl! You help, swinging that sickle, dreaming of being a warrioress."

We must've read the same books. "I canoe. More than most fishermen, I s'pose."

"A child of the vines paddling about only the gods know where. Will you show me where you saw the Gorsuka prints?"

"S'pose so. When?"

"Tonight."

I went for the window but corrected myself.

"When will the shaman be around?" I said, closing the door behind us. "Still want to ask 'im a few."

But she said nothin'. Niesuri Qell wasn't accustom to talkin' to poor folk. She was also beautiful, more demandin' than Mama on a bad day, and the first real friend I'd ever made. The demandingness came from bein' the daughter of Murgle Qell, the commissioner.

Excited didn't hold a candle to how I felt soon after. I'd take her to Pauthor's, where, for once, I'd have another pleasant face in my canoe.

How frogs change during their life—that's what I'd be reminded of later. Things appear one way, then someday they're that way no longer.

)(

You would have thought, with all the gear strapped about her, we were goin' to siege a damn castle. Her ropes and canteens hung ready as the night fog settled.

"Ready to tear off some Apraz?" she said from her dock, out from under a dark bonnet.

We were hardly the pair, her outfitted as she was and me covered in the mess left from helpin' Mama play catch-up. Mama didn't wanna talk about why she'd been gone when I'd woken up, and I didn't wanna ask. "Where to, yerr majesty?"

"Majesty? No, just the daughter of an unimpressive man who has mildly impressive responsibilities. And to where you saw the prints." Hoppin' down in my canoe and grabbin' a paddle, she said, "Shaman Rehton says they are the most mysterious animal in our swamp."

"Spent most my years not believin' in 'em. S'pose fairies are real too now. *Those* I wouldn't mind seein'!"

"I'll roll a loaded dice I know another thing you wouldn't mind *seein'*."

She lurched forward and dug into her satchel. Out came a little cage, and blinkin' from within was a glowin' frog. I took the cage from Niesuri and saw there was a second glower, cowerin' behind the one lookin' at me.

"One for me, one for you," she said.

She didn't waste no time. Niesuri went first. The bright flash lit her face. I went next. It had been a few days since my last frog, and I'd grown accustom to the wild big ones that blasted you to heaven's shores before scurryin' away. This nippit wasn't terrible, but what had me smilin' far more was how Niesuri kept lookin' at me. Like I was supper and she was a little hungry.

"All these mud huts and iron towers," she said. "They all should be brought to sunder. In the mud of the earth is where we all belong. This—" She grabbed a leafy twig that hung low. "—this is where we were meant to be."

I was fixin' to ask her to hush her rant when I saw the top of Pauthor's cabin, but when she saw it too she did all the hushin' that was necessary.

It was a wonder of the swamp. In the spanse of a day and night, mud and wind and cow hooves had messed things up so that hardly a print could be made out. Edgin' our way to the cabin like gigglin' schoolgirls, that paw print under the window was the only one left, its outline a squiggly memory holdin' leaves and renewed muck. She leaned so far in it I thought she was lookin' to kiss the damn thing.

"*This* is it?" she then said.

I felt myself shrinkin'. "It looked better last night."

"No wonder they're so hard to find," she said, lookin' about, fiddlin' with her shoulder straps.

The idea of fillin' that little cage again was makin' its way out my mouth when I saw her eyes. The old hermit's torches blazed to needle heads in 'em. She was lookin' right past me. When I turned to see what in the world had grabbed her so, all I could make out in that blackness were a few lonely lanterns.

"I want to investigate," she chirped. "Let's go."

"Yes, your grace," I snipped, but her fingers that caressed me got me steppin'.

As we got closer to the lanterns, I saw 'em to be two low-hangers on the stern of a one-man raft. By some unspoken girl language, Niesuri knew to stop paddlin' and let me glide us in. Her head, starin' forward and set to orange, I put dead middle of the lights.

The raftmen's back was to us. He was a willowy, watery sot, balancin' a spear as best he could in both hands. His raft was floatin' toward a fallen tree. I docked us against its sidelong trunk right as he did.

"Watch this," I said to Niesuri, crawlin' past her. The trunk was like a dock, one I made my way down until I was clear past the man.

I don't know why I did it. I found myself thinkin' about her touch as we'd left the hermit's cabin. How it made somethin' in me move. I shucked off my dress. By the time the frogger laid eyes on the enchanted, womanly spirit, I was wavin' like the lit tongue of a candle. Though I could see his face thaw and gawk, the silhouette behind 'im, watchin' in silence from my canoe, that's who I was really barin' all for.

He took off his britches, then he fell face first in the water.

Niesuri and I climbed onto the raft from both sides, gigglin' somethin' awful.

"Check his basket, quick," I said, lookin' over my shoulder. He'd hadn't come up yet. Tryin' to meet me out on the trunk proved too hard for 'im, and I was hopin' climbin' back onto his raft would be a tough one too.

"Nothing. No frogs," she said. "No loot."

I kicked his spear into the water. When we scrammed, we took his net and lanterns but dumped the lights when the sling stones started to come crackin' in.

In the bog there are floatin' islands. Mud and generations of weeds that grow in clumps you could build cabins on. We banked on one, far away from the stupid frogger, greased slick in our sweat.

"Some time you have out here," she said, pantin', findin' a

patch of dry weeds to nestle in. "Frolicking with the frogs and slithering with the reptiles."

"And ain't nobody know it but me." It sounded silly and extra poor, even to me. But as I leaned on my paddle, it may have well been a staff, and I some loved druid bein' told all my long-waited feel-goods.

"Show me what else you do that nobody else knows."

She jumped when I lunged forward to unsheathe the knife from her belt, and was still as bark moss while I cut into my arm.

"Does it hurt?" she said, sidlin' her way toward me. Before I'd answered, she pressed her cool lips against the slice, her mouth meetin' the hot runnin' blood. When I offered her the blade, she batted it away. Eyes like a croc's shinin' under the moon returned to a gigglin' girl's. "Blood of the ordinary attracts the extraordinary."

Quotin' a line from that high-brow Vandahl captured me, sure. I was just about to open my mouth on account of its insultin' usage when right then a huge flash of frog-light erupted on the far side of the island.

Do the gods favor the wicked? I'd snatched that dunked frog-ger's net for no reason other than it bein' there. Now, because of it, I caught in one cast one of the largest scores in all my days. Tyin' off the net to some cattails, they could rest in place—after I'd plucked a nice fat one, of course.

"So," she said, makin' me remember it wasn't just me and my stash. "Ever gone down on a woman?"

I spun 'round to see she'd taken off her britches. She was sprawled out on the grass, bottom arched up, her head turned, lookin' back at me. She looked like a squirrel on a branch, flattened low to evade a hawk. But not so flat I couldn't see her fingers, rubbin' the place she told me I needed to kiss.

Yeah, a squirrel—we must have looked like two of 'em hemmed together. What they look like when that love chase around the tree trunk ends. Growin' up I'd given myself to men for all sorts of reasons, not least among them the desire to feel somethin'. But it was as if inside me there was a flame, one that the greatest efforts of men couldn't flicker. She grabbed onto hunks of grass and pulled herself down low. Swamp water bubbled up. I found my footin' in a patch of mud and pushed my face into her.

"Eat it like you fucking mean it," she growled. "This is seriously all you got?"

"I'll bite you."

She took my reaction as a good thing. I wasn't sure how I meant it. But any other would-be mumblin' was soon lost between her legs.

Funny how down there she smelled the same, yet so different. *Every petal a star*, I think Vandahl wrote. She wanted me down there, but when I crawled up to kiss her, she was distant. I chalked it up to her bein' sensitive to the scent of her own juice, though it made her pushin' me back no less awkward.

"Lilac as in amber," she said, standin' with her britches around her ankles, takin' a drink from her canteen. The frogs lit up behind me, showin' an' shinin' how wet I'd made her.

Confused by her lilac thing, I resided to sittin' and watchin' 'er as she stared out into the black. I tackled her. It was her turn. Though I was stronger, she wiggled free and clasped her thighs around my ears, securin' a second go. This time I could look up, past her sweaty clothes and the ropes crossin' on top of 'em. Her face showed I was doin' it well, but somehow not well enough.

"Move mountains with mouse mist," she said.

I thought I'd recognized *that* one; some verse out of a poetry book I must of glanced at a time or two. Why she was sayin' this garbage was lost on me.

I tied down the net, but not before pickin' out a frog and runnin' it through with her knife. It lit bright and we shared its blast, placin' our hands on it no different than soothsayers on one of their confounded conjurin' boards.

I watched as Niesuri waded out into the water. I was unable to move, even when I saw a big roll engulf her before dissipatin' back to cool languid black.

"They are leaving," she said.

"Well, I reckon by what I've seen of late, they'll be back."

She turned and looked at me. Steppin' out and liftin' me up to plant a real kiss on me for the first time: "They sure will."

)(

The nights that followed were a blur of zaps, more sex, and more angry men. No raft, canoe, or floatin' hovel was safe. Havin' a cache of frogs to head to gave us a direct route come dusk, but by the wee hours we'd bumped off and careened into every trunk, stump, and weed-line, from the northbound road clear across the bog's western shore.

By the time the sun turned the docks mottled brown again, litters of night prowlers had been capsized, seduced, looted, or all three. Rumors sprang: rival addicts were disruptin' nightly pursuits, or that graveside cult had done messed up good, evokin' two sportive ghosts, appearin' as young women, both out to wreak havoc on the world. Niesuri seemed to enjoy the adventurin' so much she lost her interest in what may or may not be swimmin' below us.

I was pretty sure those Gorsukas were long gone. With all the flappin' arms we'd sent into the water, those creatures would have had a buffet. Even a trip back to Pauthor's shown the Pelat fence mended, not a print in the mud or a cursin' foreigner puffin' a pipe. When I wasn't droolin' and dazed, it made me shiver, thinkin' what monstered under us as we giggled in our rockin' canoe. But they seemed to me good and gone.

"You were right," I said one night. "Gone like summer."

"Not right enough," she said. "Piss on books and studyin' charts! Those beasts have magical powers—and not like those farmer-doping frogs you're so fond of. I mean *real* power."

When most the Qell tribe began their yearly uprootin' to spend autumn in Oxghorde, a roof-rattlin' fight broke out between Niesuri and her daddy. At the end of it, our commissioner watched with a quiverin' lip as he and his lumpy delegation brought Niesuri to our doorstep. In a gamblin' town such as ours, I reckon if the pageant had gone on any longer, the delegation and myself along with 'em would have started placin' bets on who was going to faint from disbelief first: Mama or Murgle Qell.

Niesuri had seen the wild side of the swamp—my side, and she wasn't leavin'. Her studies with Shaman Rehton would continue, she'd said. Niesuri moved into my room, but did so sulky an' sullen, not the bright sleepover I'd imagined, or hoped for.

Weeks passed. My kisses were still met, but even I, collector of one friend, knew our whatever-it-was was becomin' more one-sided each day.

Us bein' lovers was somethin' we vowed to keep a secret. And we did so. Our success, however, didn't stop Mama from slammin' cabinet doors, stompin' around like a Pelat cow, and huffin' and puffin' like she'd come down with swamp rattle. Maybe Mama had really lost her mind a bit 'cause of Daddy's big vanish. No matter how many times I told her my friend was only stayin' until her uppity family got bored lookin' at red and yellow leaves, Mama'd fly into slurs like some buried treasure of ours would be found out an' plundered.

⟊

No seasons in the bog. What some call autumn and winter passed, as did the first days of spring. My room briefly became a flurry. Niesuri's dresses had to be hung just right, there were more sets of her boots than days between new moons—and then I was reacquainted with my water-stained floor.

Briefly a flurry—the Qells fled the Oxghorde winter and reclaimed their rebellin' heiress. It wounded me how happy Niesuri was to leave. She hopped in their polished canoe like a fox. She'd been happy to go, sittin' on her chests, talkin' with her even happier dad. But none were happier than Mama, who danced a high-elbowed jig then swore me to never see that high and mighty bitch ever again.

My sneakin' was soon put back into use. The Qell place was the only cabin I'd ever seen bigger than the shaman's. With iron door frames and bowin' girders of the same, the loomin' block that owned the window I'd shimmy in to see Niesuri was more an unmovable ship than a home.

Niesuri found more and more reasons why I couldn't come back to her bed, and maybe that's why the paddle to see her seemed to stretch on the nights I was lucky enough to be invited. Mid-spring got me to harvestin', while Niesuri probably began primpin' her dress to become the Municipal One's dissatisfied queen.

As spring waned, my worries ate me whole. We still met, petted and ground against the other, but her insistence on spoutin' that poetry afterwards finally impaled me. If I'd been able to blast a death glow of my own, I would've lit up the bog. I'd finally found what she'd been pullin' from. It was *The Ballad of Zenciline*, about a high and mighty bitch who waxed on and on about a love that droves of suitors tried and failed to give. She didn't love me, perhaps never did. I was nothin' more than my canoe and paddles, used to liven up her life a bit.

It was the last days of spring. I'd convinced myself she'd found a new lover, one who could please her so easily in all the ways I never could. While Murgle Qell was one room over, rehearsin' his speech for the Party of the Rains, I found Niesuri's perfumed, muddy clothes heaped in a corner on her floor. It was mud caked on from adventurin'. She got hot when I reminded her she told me she'd been housebound an' sick all week.

"Look who wants to argue," she said. "The simpleton knows formal debate like I know poverty. Go meander in the high grass, will you."

)(

I sat quiet in my canoe. A tree had fell, like the one I'd ran out on our first night together. Its canopy half out the water, I hid deep in its Witch Bush. She'd been glowin' when I slogged away, and I was willin' to suffer waking up here at summer's end just to know what she was doin' behind my back.

A weariness had claimed me. At first I forgave it as depression, but now even shuttin' my eyes, I'd begun to see my flu-driven dream.

I opened my eyes to find her standin' on her family's dock, lit by nearin' torches.

She wore the muddy cloak I'd seen crumpled on her floor. She shrugged it onto her shoulders the way a bird manages rain on its plume, and like some birds, her dress, more befittin' a ceremony, was as ornate as poached feathers.

I sobbed into my hands. Whoever she was steppin' down into that long canoe for, this stranger deserved her finest…and the cruel end of my paddle. I chewed on this while hardly noticin' all the hooded shadows in the canoe, usin' their own paddles to carry Niesuri away.

Stowin' my tears, I emerged from the Witch Bush and trailed behind. Their torches burned above 'em all on poles, makin' orange the waters and givin' me a beacon as I paddled in silence.

They led me to a rise of land, a ribbon of mud they docked against. This had to be the animal cult, Niesuri and likely that shaman lauded members. I could step onto the mud and proclaim myself a recruit. If it was my rustic simplicity that disappointed her, joinin' 'em would surely prove my willingness and devotion. Devotion to her, even if I had to become one of their worshipped beasts to do it.

They got out and formed half a circle. Sure as death, "Gorsuka, Gorsuka," they began chantin', over and over an' over again.

I glided into nearby shadow. In the mud, I could see all the prints, those that were human, and the ones that weren't.

From their canoe, they pulled out two big bundles. One they unrolled to reveal a totem pole layin' within.

It was like kids playin' make believe. They continued chantin', uprightin' this totem in the mud. The totem was a crocodilish thing, sittin' on its haunches, more like an obedient dog than a god. Its round, lizardy face had jewels for eyes, reflectin' in the torches.

My emotions tripped each other, racin' in my heart. Fear of what was likely gonna crawl out of the swamp, and somethin' else, somethin' that wasn't fear. I counted eight people, all masked in the darkness of their hoods. Then there was Niesuri, hood down, busy untyin' the second bundle.

I gasped when a young girl crawled out, languid and dreamin'. Laid onto the mud under the totem, she had to be under the spell of some potent drug.

Niesuri held up somethin' and then shook it. I recognized it—that tambourine thing from back at the shaman's. After a moment of rattlin', she dropped it and crawled on top of the girl. The passion with which she kissed her almost brought me to vomit; the turn of her head, the ecstasy that closed eyes can show, the gleam of spit on lips. Only the girl's lifelessness served as the stitch that kept me from explodin'.

There is a memory. I don't see it as my eyes must've, but as someone else perched high above me. I remember wonderin' if this girl—some poor urchin who probably lived in a lean-to against a grave—if her role had once been intended to be my own, and if Niesuri'd had a change of heart, and all her scorn was a way to push me away, to save me.

Every member of that cult jumped back, one fallin' right over in the canoe. The Gorsuka had emerged. The beast licked its lips and stepped fully onto the mud. It licked its lips like a person would, then ate the girl in one gulp. A thrill in me was cut short when I realized I'd screamed.

The cult and the monster looked at me at the same time. In all of this, Niesuri's eyes met my own. When she'd seen what she'd summoned out of the bog, her eyes were full of fire, her mouth wide like one seein' for the first time what they've wished for all their life. Now, her eyes were cold. Wanting to save me, she hadn't.

I fled. I fled as the muscles in my arms gathered acid. My canoe burst through bush and debris. In a madman's sprint, I reached home with my lungs on fire.

)(

When I awoke, to my surprise, it wasn't the beginnin' of fall but only a sliver of time since I'd toppled over outside our door. I was in my bed, still in my clothes covered in mud and grime, the sweat still beadin' on my brow.

Niesuri? Why was she walking through the front door?

"Mama!" I shrieked, jumping out of bed.

"Yes, baby," Mama said. She was wrapped in towel, her hair wet. "I am here." Grave was her voice, more so than my collapse or even Niesuri's return should've made grave.

I was over Niesuri; she could feed half of Amden to those foul beasts for all I cared, as long as I never had to hear her voice or see that insufferable egg of a face.

My chuckle filled the room. Gorsukas were real.

The paw prints finally made sense at least, though not much else did. The way Mama and Niesuri stood, like bookends for a twisted reader bent on bent women. They almost seemed to hear my thoughts. Mama and Niesuri separated the way scolded children may after gettin' caught fiddlin' their bits. And how calmly I spoke.

I said, "Looks like your pets are real." I went to the rear of the room to tear off and throw down my clothes. "And *this* one is finally off its leash, and for good."

But Niesuri wasn't done bein' Niesuri. "Just can't help your-self," she said, "can you? We are done. Nosin' in my affairs, ruining what you couldn't possibly fathom! Why, with your bark-gnawing ways." Whatever she was goin' to say next was outdone by a new thought that appeared behind her face. It was a face I figured she'd make. "No room for secrets with *us*. I think we should go ahead and tell her."

Who? Mama?! Niesuri's voice began to turn my blood cold as a crocodile's. What now—after her toy, her fuck mule, had enough, she thought only fittin' to wreck its love with the only person it has in the whole wide world? Our way was behavior Mama could never understand.

Mama stood still as that totem. She must have already known, and that knowin' had destroyed her.

My hands became fists. I flew into a howlin' rage, causin' Niesuri to step back. When she did, that—balial—that thing she'd used to call forth her scaled giant, the instrument I'd remembered seein' at the shaman's the day we'd met rattled against her hip. My eyes were drawn to it as if it had whispered my name.

Mama was sure to join me in finally dealin' with Niesuri. Mama was sure to storm over and tear her limb from limb. It surprised me then to see Mama runnin', but not to Niesuri, but to me...to stop me.

The room was squeezin', practically suffocatin' me. What had been my yellin' deluded into grunts, then into growls. I lunged at Niesuri. In the heat of disagreement we had once attacked the other in girlish combat, but this time she felt as insignificant as a straw-stuffed doll. Her entrails were raked across our floor with a hand that had grown large, and green. Somewhere in this hellish scene Niesuri's mouth was ripped wide by a lone claw. I heard my voice hiss, *"Lilac as in amberrrrrr."*

It was night still, revealin' itself through our open door. Mama was lookin' at the carnage. I rose to my feet. She licked her lips and rolled her eyes at me.

"We were lovers." It muttered from my lips without thought. Despite the ghastly scene, I squirmed more as I waited for Mama's reaction. The squirmin' was all mine.

"I've been around humans long enough to know, baby."

Though I knew I should've been repulsed to my knees by the blood and mangled face and chunks that still twitched, I was nothin' of the sort. I noticed a vague sensation like hunger as I willed myself to begin gatherin' Niesuri. And *humans*? "What happened, Mama?"

"Your daddy did get eaten by a swamp monster, and I think you know that now." I was lookin' down at what was in my hands, clutchin' snapped ribs and half-digested bile. They were my hands again. "It's just your mother *was* the monster. *Is* a monster, as you are, baby."

They say drinkers suffer from delirium when deprived of the jug. There was for sure a frogger's equal. After Mama was admitted into the loony house, I'd pluck me a fat one, or two fat ones. I'd simply passed out again, surely, and done so with powerful hallucinations.

But Mama was determined: "Our kind don't usually hide our truth from our kin."

"Then why did you?" I heard myself sayin' as my throat gulped down a cry.

"If I'd raised *you* on the truth, the whole truth, you wouldn't of owned it with the sense of pride our kind does. In the summers we become our true selves. Been this way forever. We need the bog, as we need our secret. You think a skittish town, here or elsewhere, wouldn't impale us on stakes the moment we showed back up as humble sights like Mortha or Matina? No, my daughter, you would've told the first limpin' town folk you could've grabbed ahold of. Our secret would've begun to unravel. That would end us, all of us."

"Makes no sense." I felt a surge that I thrust forward. "If so, all our women eat their men? And what made me so damn different?"

She keened her eyes. "You know your kind better than you think, Matina. Our males, once they've done their part, we eat 'em. You'll soon see—again, you could say. They don't grow any bigger. Just us, baby."

Standing amidst the human slop I'd stopped collectin', I restated my second absurd question.

"You spent so much time fallin' through the parchment of their books," she replied, "and oglin' at their ways, their psyche rubbed off on you. Them, with their rat-colony neediness, their validations drainin' no slower than a leaky pot." She shut the front door. "Those damn books. I shoulda known better. They made you long for the father you never met, and all the waywardness comin' with it. Such human longin' damaged you, girl."

I had one last objection; how, in this preposterous fiction, would the youngins survive if they didn't transform right along with their daddy-eatin' mamas? Then she made my stomach cold. "You transform too. The flu, baby. The flu where you 'fall asleep' and wake up when summer's gone."

It was as if I was bein' spun an' whirled by a tornado. Guilt for not believin' her—sheer terror for what it meant to—and a glimmer of the most wild exhilaration that came with the planks of my world bein' pulled out from underneath me.

At last, I said, "So, what? We're like some scaly werewolf?"

She glanced at our bookshelf with a smirk. "Don't transform as often as werewolves."

The room was closin' in on me again. I had to escape; out of our cabin, the bog, Rehleia, and perhaps the world itself. As my feet splashed the waters, I began to fade. I felt what I'd felt all those times I'd sunk into my dream, though this was no dream. I heard Mama yell, "Don't! Don't you tell 'em!" as I dove under.

𝒳

Power. Powerful. Lightning that bursts in the skies, thrust into reptilian veins.

Denizens in the vast coolness that the humans called things like *river bed*—those soft, pink two-leggers in the far-off cities knew no community as the metropolis of the water world. Schools of fish hummed past me. Beautiful glowing frogs pulsed the upper shores into dazzling symphony as I shouldered through ancient sediments.

In the channel's depths, I was met by the crocodiles, lower cousins, lying themselves flat near the sunken trees and trunks they resembled. *Giant* crawfish—once my youthful fear, when I walked with two legs—those armored bugs darted and dispersed as I used my great tail.

I knew all I had known as Matina, and I knew that I had always known my…double life, the moment I transformed back to pureness. Only the blackness bequeathed by retrograding to human form fed me such queer illusions of what was for so long my reality.

I ruminated on such things as I emerged onto Pauthor's mud and broke down the Pelat's fence to help myself to a cow. I ruminated on such things as the night gave way to day and I swam amongst the swaying weeds and watery caves that were my birthright. The day's light showed my realm—not the teethy abyss the humans spun tales over, but a calm, tranquil realm, one whose invitation adept ears could hear.

As night above began conquering day, I chased down a tasty crawfish. I knew it was still my favorite, now that I was back. I would have loved to have seen the terrified fishermen when they saw all the bubbles, my bubbles, erupting up from all my laughing: I hated shellfish as a two-legged girl.

𝕏

I had no idea why I was naked. There was the vague recollection of bein' asked a question where I reluctantly answered "yes." Now I sat on one of Amden proper's docks with my head between my knees. I was wet, like I'd fallen into the water, and maybe that was why I was cryin'.

Maybe I'd happened on a bad frog. Instead of frolickin' on my tippy toes, some rare afflicted one sent me to the wilderness crazed. I'd perhaps shed my clothes, but then again—

"The swamp flu," I whispered. "The sleep." Why did the thought of this irritate me? It was as if some name was on the tip of my tongue, but every time it felt close to revealin' itself, it slipped away.

Mama and I had a reckonin' comin'. And Niesuri...good and gone, sure, but the nightmare I'd had...or *thought* I'd had. My mind was mush, and all I'd been through lately surely made it so. Right? I convinced myself so, but it didn't bid goodbye to a feelin' like I'd been taken out of my skin.

The music and laughter from the Party of the Rains at last pulled me from my sobbin'. I would learn later that Murgle Qell spared everyone his speech to head up a search party. Our home would be ransacked and burned to the ground. But first, on this night, I dried my face and searched for my clothes. I would go to the party as I'd always wished to. Dance with my fellow swamp folk. "Begone, you nasty swamp flu," I said, proppin' up higher my growin' sense of pride. Then a hand grabbed the back of my neck.

My head smacked against the dock. "On yerr back, little dove," a man said.

"Aww, lookie, Norb," a second one said, low and mean. "Little lass doesn't have a date fer the party?"

"That's okay," said a third. "We don't care much for crowds. Do we, Norb?"

The man pinnin' me to the planks let out a laugh that stank like beer. "Nope. No, we don't."

I kicked and pleaded when they flipped me over. I gasped when my legs were grabbed an' spread, and a rigid cock entered me where one never should. I thought I was passin' out from the pain, until I knew it was somethin' else. Grunts and hoarse laughter faded, then grew louder as my hands grew. With them my back, and my neck, feelin' in one instant as thick as a tree. Laughter turned to screams. Screams turned to crunching.

The dock creaked under my weight. I—the real *I*—slipped off and back into my waters with a full belly.

)(

I, who had just felt those tears the girl had cried, felt the violations her body had suffered, swam low through the muck and swampweed as Matina. Whoever that girl had been, wielding my name without a clue as to her true power, I knew—as the sounds above grew louder—that this naïve little human was gone forever.

With a full heart, those stickly little beings would meet what—no, *who* a fringe of them already worshipped.

The Party of the Rains: as a human girl with fits of amnesia, I'd spun this drudgery into yarns of gold. How hilarious my new senses made my former life's obscurities. What I'd once imagined as glowing tents and fairyland was nothing more magnificent than if a herd of cows had learned to play the fiddle and drink their herder's beer.

I waded toward the ruckus, breaking the water's surface with only my big, yellow eyes, the rise of my back, and the top of an ever-useful tail. My keen sight was restored, able to pick out lone stumblers from what had to be a quarter of a mile. Those who worshipped the Gorsuka were in attendance. I now recalled every face.

More to my surprise was the sizable group of Pelats. Mingling about the tents and Murgle's empty stage, these little cow providers had decided this was the year Amden would accept its new inhabitants. It was a charming notion, I clearly thought, thinking clearer still that the town would likely blame them for what was about to transpire.

Bonfires lit eyes ablaze. Not yet stupefied on wine, partygoers gazing at the water cocked their heads when orange orbs flashed toward them. I submerged to make my grand entry.

Now I have said this night showed me the full caliber of my senses, and this was never truer than when Mortha tackled me before I could roar onto land.

Teeth sunk into my back. My belly smashed into the deepest sediment. The burst of air forced from my lungs must have knocked backward any who stared from the water's edge. Below the surface, she clawed at my eyes and fought to hook my hind legs with her own. I didn't question why.

The moment she rammed me, the message was spoken. But we spoke not in ways that you, a human, may know. When a Gorsuka touches another, our scales are more than the familiar rub of kin, or of brother, but a conduit between ancient minds who spoke before there were words.

Mortha wouldn't allow our kind to be revealed. To her, I was "reckless, as destructive in girlish youth as in true form." It was no matter, whether I wanted to destroy all in sight or retrograde back onto two legs and dazzle them with high tales of transformation; it would be the beginning of the end. Mortha, who was charged by the "blood in her bones," had to act for the good of the Gorsukan. The death of her daughter was horrid, the death of her species worse.

She wept as she bit and clawed, all the more when I told her she was right.

One slip was all I needed. Mortha's hind leg kicked wildly,

hoping to wrap up my own, thus sprawling me wide and pinning me hopelessly to the bottom. Matching the wheeling of her kicks, I was able to gain a hook. From my memory as a girl, I imitated the acrobatics of negotiating vines of Apraz. Pressing up with my fore limbs, I ignored the lacerations I was accruing, for I'd cut myself plenty as a human girl. Then I trapped her leg and used it as a fulcrum. I flipped Mortha. She disappeared into a storm of disturbed muck, but not before blasting me across the snout with her tail.

Desperate for air, I shot for the surface. When my head broke the water I gulped in fresh, whooping bales of hot night air. Teeth sunk into my tail. Shouts from the tents and docks were drowned out by the *swish* of water as I was pulled back down.

The exchange of bites and strikes was furious. I knew I'd hurt her, how bad I couldn't say. But for all my greatest attacks, I felt myself slipping.

She overpowered my efforts. My bites—she lunged out of their range. My tail—constricted by hers like a snake. My claws—insignificant to her mighty back scales. At last I begged for mercy, that I'd be no trouble, but we both knew I was lying. Dying wet is what anyone born in the bog expects, just not like this.

Belly to belly, her jaws around enough of my throat, I was to be drowned. In our melee, she'd found a rarity: a rock jutting up out the swamp bottom. Perhaps frozen by pain and deprived of air, my eyes saw nothing, but I knew I was being lifted to be slammed back down upon it.

When Mortha let go, I'd half expected to rise and look at one another with human faces. A mother's love, they say. Lifting my head, I strained to see the shimmering lights of party fires. I was under her, and we were right under the surface! So close to one dock I could feel the hurry of boots.

Scrambling for air, I found I was still seized by Mortha's legs. Then a spear went past my head. Another one, then another sank below me. From under the water and her massive girth, Mortha's back sounded like a drum being beaten by an ill-tempered child. With no intentions to be clever, I thrust up against her belly, sucking my lungs full. What I'd done accidently was give my mother's attackers good reason to believe she was bursting right out of the swamp to confront their cruel weaponry.

Mesmerized by the "swamp monster" and all its violent thrashing, not a soul saw me while I caught my breath. I sunk back down and wrapped my tail around the rock. Then I looked up, and I waited.

I learned a few seasons later how a giant back emerged after all the bubbles—the ones the partygoers swore contained terrible growls when they broke free. I also learned that beer, frogs, and liquor don't stop the spear from stinging, nor its aim to be true—especially when they come hurling down by the dozens.

The later spears would be tied to ropes. Before Mortha was dragged up to be ogled at and butchered, she reached out with a paw. It was searching, not in the way of a predator or a combatant, nor was it mindless twitching. It was the call of a mother. With most of her life already gone, my merciful bite to her neck went unchallenged. I ripped into her with a precise fang, but not before a spear ripped through my cheek. I sunk my fang deep and then tore it free. Her blood spewed.

She was hoisted up to burden the dock. The last I saw of her was the tip of her tail, then that too was fetched by a hurled spear.

Beaten, weary, I swam off. In the nursing blackness of the channel depths, I would regain my strength. Then I would meet the others.

When I bit down, Mortha let me know all, all that she'd said I *had* to know now. The town folk wouldn't just kill, but torture us. They'd catch us in human form, blame us for all their sorrows, impale us on the stake, and all would be lost. Mortha hadn't just been a concerned Gorsuka, but had been Queen of the Gorsuka, dutifully protecting her kind.

Swimming the direction she told me, I indeed recalled the pillars of submerged oak leading to the meeting place. Passing the last of these pillars, it occurred to me that I was now queen.

I watched our circle form. My fellow females flattened against the bottom, our few and greyish males swimming down to appear slight beside us. Once all were settled, I was welcomed. On a lone rock, not much different than the one she almost broke me on, I took up what had been Mortha's long-held perch.

From this moss-covered throne, I weighed my life and its truths. It was true I was never good enough for Niesuri as a human girl. It was also true I'd actually been the real princess out of our pair all along. My heart hurt how ironic it was, how she'd likely love me now more than ever. Then I felt that hurt wash away.

I was Matina. As I returned all the sly smiles facing me in my watery court, I knew I was back with my kind.

Disavowing humans would come in doubling bounds of joy, and they would have to toil with a new hate and fear in their bog. The new Gorsuka Queen had remembered her appetite for their precious frogs.

THE HERMIT

Cut 'em down,
an' stack 'em high,
Fill our purse
'til the day we, too, die.

—Song of the Rigl Farmer

Before Matina's perch on the Gorsukan Stone, another tale was unfurling amongst the swamp thistle.

The lusting of the spirit—of *a* spirit—is the tale to be told, one where consequence begat consequence, and doing so would not only affect the queen but the lowly humans above her, their ways, their town, the bog itself.

Amden Bog is the home of an evil, or so the adage goes. What else could the world call those who violate nature, tear governances eternally binding, ready to devour the hopes and breath of the breathing, all in the dark hope to, too, breathe again?

But, as is usually the case where corruptions reign above a water's line, the shedding of blood can never be relegated to a single, simple perpetrator. And the perpetrators we can touch, wield, or eat have a way of being talked about first.

So, there is some truth to the adage that Amden Bog is the source of *all* evils. That is, of course, if by *all evils* you're referring to all that's happened in the province of Rehleia.

When the Municipal One was still being called the Conqueror, his blood-soaked title became all the more credible after his campaign discovered that which fed and refueled his warring: the Rigl mushroom.

The progeny of the Moliahenna River running to lay with an ancient lowland, Amden Bog teems with boatmen busily fishing, battling beasts, and when out of the water, harvesting Rigl in the bog's black mud.

Their stems tall as a man and sturdy as spears, their caps dull and red as rusted shields, a fungi which grow only in the bog was hewn, stacked, and wagoned off to the ever-expanding front lines.

It surely wasn't for their taste. Bickering was unified, from armored louts busily braining woodland rebels to horsemen negotiating the quicksands of Azad. The hardtack that resulted from the Rigl tasted like a dog, menaced by some disease, had squatted over a bemolded loaf of bread.

Though one could get from Amden to the city of Oxghorde without having to unsaddle their horse, Oxghordians had once wondered why their water-logged neighbors would come up to trade skins and croc meat for coin, but didn't stuff their carts with breads and apples and all else a dismal swamp was unable to provide. A mystery no longer. While unappealing to the eye or the gut, one Rigl, with little to no preparation, could last a man for years. Ten thousand, an army, and for a decade.

But the wars had ended, and those who dwelled within the bog's watery edge had returned to their ways.

X

Orloc Quithot's canoe prowled, low and slim, separating another patch of reeds. The night may have hidden the protruding logs, if he hadn't known them all. Some looked like the heads of marsh creatures, others their backs.

He was more than just a Rigl farmer. Orloc's least concern was navigating his own bog, capsizing to commune with crocodiles. Between his feet lay his rotten net. In his hands, he pushed and dug with a pole, propelling him onward.

The mild brown of his skin and garb were as insignificant as any single tree amongst the sprawl of oak, ash, and cypress. But his eyes were jeweled, deep beads holding their simmering gleam.

Night was the only way. A swollen moon had long broken over the trees, its light reflecting off the rumples made by the canoe. By way of a break in the cypress, Orloc entered a moss-roofed lagoon.

He saw the glowing.

Pulsing in the shallows, lunar yellow drew him. His dry tongue ran across dry lips. He lifted the pole's spearhead out of the muck. Orloc, unable to blink or breathe, brought the long stalk of the spear up and then drove it down.

Laughing with a sounds fit for a madman, Orloc lifted his spear amidst the bright splash. Up came a large frog, kicking, impaled on the end of the blade. The size of a cabbage, the frog's belly erupted in yellow light. Orloc pulled in the spear the way a sailor would pull in a rope. Clutched between shaking hands, the frog's dying flashes blazed in the farmer's eyes.

){

Pauthor Quithot hated allegory, but if he was going to be shackled to it, his brushes could at least create paintings that weren't entirely terrible. His portfolio wasn't ready yet, or *gallery ready* as the PCA scroll had read. Fortunately, the Pelliul College of Art only required four completed works to enter its halls, have them scrutinized, then begin the glorious torment of learning learn from the masters.

As the moon dropped beyond his hut, lethargy set into his bones. All the great artists seemed to have been victims to the demon of irony. His inclusion into such a reluctant brood gave him hope, so much so that being born both with fen-lung syndrome and in Amden Bog only moderately hindered his ambition.

Pauthor put his final touches on the final painting's midground. The farthest thing from genius, it compelled him nonetheless, extolling the dramatic fate of a clown.

In the scene depicted, the wretched doofus was caught in an egregious slip. The clown held a looking glass. Though his painted-face bore a comic expression, the reflection in the glass, set to meet the eyes of the viewer, showed that he was crying. The clown's shoes were not just slipping, but were tearing a hole in the earth. Tiny silhouettes, with their arms flailing and fingers splayed, fell into the fire-lit gorge. Near Pauthor's signature, a single figure clung to an overhang of amber and blazing lemon.

When the front door swung open it did so with a rattle and bang fit to knock the snakes out of the thatching and onto the rafters. To Pauthor's fortune, he had already swept his ceremonial final brushstroke, avoiding what would doubtless have been a ribbon of unwanted black over an apple red shoe.

"Paulie boy," Orloc slurred, then shambled in without shutting the door. "Whatcha doin?"

"Just finished," Pauthor said, shutting the door, hiding the tired smirk he'd once felt guilt over for condemning his father's oft-inebriation. "Gig a good one?"

Orloc was on the floor. Pauthor braced himself as, after the usual sentimental quips and slobbers, his father rose and took a sudden turn to seriousness.

"Abso—floggin—mazin', boy," Orloc said, swaying in front

of the painting. Pauthor shrugged off the hand that had flopped on his shoulder.

"It's for the PCA."

"Of course I like it. Yerr mamma was quite the artist. Still is, I 'spose. You shine to her side."

"It's for the PCA."

"Follow those dreams, Paulie. It's all we—"

"Got. Yeah, I know."

"The whole worlds as big as you make it, son." Orloc proceeded into incoherence.

Beefing up the fire and stowing his brushes, simple weariness settled on the young artist. Orloc had returned to a favored spot on the floor. As his father's snoring deepened into flapping growls, before blowing out the last candle, Pauthor read his coveted admissions scroll one last time. Soon he would be leaving the bog, and its fetidness.

$$\text{)(}$$

In midday heat, amongst the steams, all manner of bog beast struggle to find shade. Even the Blood Suckers and the ill-natured Winged Scourge took refuge from the sweltering oppression of the sun, hiding in shadows or egressing out from under the massive Rigl that Pauthor hacked down with a sickle.

Pauthor, long ago on some obscure workday that almost killed him, had put together why the boglings excelled in horticulture but had never squirted out a lone astronomer to join the celebrated heap of celestials and star-gawkers up in Oxghorde. The bog's canopies didn't so much make a plane of shadow, as that would hint at the innate superiority of light. Rather, the boa-vines and Witch Bush allowed only small green pockets of sun. The eternal gloom, especially water's edges like the front porch of the Quithot hut, was prime ground for cultivation.

Rigl, though a wispy candle to the sun compared to the war

days, was still aggressively harvested. Its stunning economy combined with its punitive taste had resulted in extensive contracts
with an assortment of minor jailhouses and pillories, but also
major incarcerators, like Pelliul's Parilgotheum and the Nilghorde
Municipal Dungeon.

Not far away, under a wide-brimmed hat, Orloc grimed with
the sweat of years. Pulling from an accompanying bucket, he
handfulled sporelings into awaiting trenches of substrate. These
trenches, long, troublesome, and never without a gang of stubborn
roots, had been Orloc's previous day's task.

Pauthor's duty today was to cut down and stack the grown
ones, or "money-makers," as Orloc called them, and in a way
that made Pauthor glad they lived in almost complete isolation.
Pauthor bent and cut and plucked and bundled as he'd done times
innumerable, and just as times innumerable, as the sun leered
down from its towerly position and tickled the Moliahenna, his
lungs were left heaving. Though tan like most boglings, Pauthor
looked how he felt: eternally gaunt.

The back door of the Quithots opened out to a flimsy boardwalk. By a short adventure, planks took them to their work,
sparing them dances around fly-swarmed pools that held bot-
toms no stick nor sounding spear could find. Drooping over the
boardwalk's rail, Pauthor had moved from his work to now stare
at his toes. He could barely breathe.

"Had that shit when I was yerr age," Orloc said, lifting himself up past Pauthor and toward the nearest water jug. Wiping
his spittle away, Pauthor's standard reply—he'd needed to leave
the swamp years ago—was halted by his father's: "Man up, son.
Swamp rattle don't kill anybody willin' to work past it."

How helpful, Pauthor thought. There was no doubt his father
was a workhorse. Get him started, and that wide-brimmed hat
would traverse clear across from one side of the toiled-over to
the other. And with this came the inevitable condescension to

all others, which was everyone, who didn't possess the virility of his trowel. But his father's rather unrestrained speech came as a surprise. Not because Orloc insisted on calling fen-lung syndrome "swamp rattle"—no, that was to be expected. It was more because, after being zapped by one of those frogs, his father's renowned silence usually lasted right up until that tattered net was being tossed into their canoe to go catch another.

Some called it *consumption*; other, more lettered types, like the Qells in Amden's drier parts, called it *transference*. Whatever the verb to transport how the land's unique and glowing denizens interacted with the less luminous, the frog's magic flashed abundantly throughout all the surrounding plots and lean-tos.

Only the gods knew what intrepid or insane bogling discovered it, but contact with those robust bellies, even upon a vapid surge, gave the holder a sensation that had been described as pleasant. The stronger ignited happiness so dizzying no man had ever been able to hold onto the frog after.

It was this distinction in potency that drew droves of farmers and crocodile hunters to abandon netting the frogs and attempt to keep them in captivity. But aside from their crafty breakouts, their captive surges were generally weak, something the local shaman diagnosed as a result of the frogs living in barrels or glass bowls, their little souls longing for slimy beds. For those who indulged too often, the effect dulled, until netting the frogs from boats and getting their surge then and there was the only solution.

For many, the frogs and their glowing surges were the lace on merry gatherings, igniting ceremonies, and sending newlyweds into awaiting bridal chambers. Yet there was another side to the discovery. Shovels lay neglected. Swamp deaths changed from the predictability of vanished croc hunters and dismemberment by giant crawfish to multiple drownings, a thing in Amden that had once been as rare as snow. The desperate could be seen at night, lanterns glowing, all lurking. From net to spear, the captor of a frog's dying jolt experienced heaven-moving euphoria.

"Orientation day is a week away," Pauthor said.

Orloc growled, tossing an empty water jug and moving to another. "Yeah, so I can be left alone to pull in the money-makers. Pelliul. Art. You sure you aren't a boy-kisser?" Here Orloc straightened and looked his son in the eye. "Yeah, I said I'd paddle you to the docks. Don't know what yerr gonna do for money, but yerr all set for wagons out."

Ж

There is an insect in the bog whose apatite-blue can brighten like lightning. Resembling a drooping dragonfly, the second of the bog's nocturnal glowers putter around the size of a crow. In flight, their abdomens light up deer trails and perch in the canopy's cancer of Witch Bush.

Pauthor was reminded of their blue as he passed a throng of Pelliul's famous street lamps. Lirelet Avenue's finest—sword swallowers, orators, painted acrobats—all greeted him. An Azadi fire-breather had moved and slithered her curves so effortlessly Pauthor only realized a few footsteps later that he'd dropped his bags. High gables and twisting flumes of jasmine rendered him a bug in a palace, one he'd be unable to paint the likeness of if he lived forever.

Were they talking to him? He paused to realize a small throng had gathered around him. He'd heard "bundle" a moment before, and thought he'd heard "another primitive." The latter he'd chalked up to the last of a departing troop of snake charmers from Pelat. "Just look at that joyous scroll," a blond man with the high cheekbones of a poet said.

"And what have we…" a young woman painted in shades of red let hang.

"Here?" Pauthor said.

As the artists burst into chimes and he sheepishly sank into his boots, one stopped laughing to remove the scroll from his hands. "Oh, cease and desist, Tinora." The tiny man flicked a wrist clad in gold ringlets. "What we have here is an admissions letter for the PCA. Don't we, star-struck one?"

Among the bullhorns that had bellowed for seemingly no other reason than darkness replacing day, Pauthor's steps lightened as fellow, though far more accomplished artists absorbed him into their glitter. He guessed one to be a thespian, but perhaps all three crossed mediums. And what wit! When Tinora had parted her braids to ask if he was hungry, her male counterparts beset her with shouts of "why for sure he is" before Pauthor had a chance to blather out his clever joust about Rigl that he'd saved for just such an occasion. A moment later, the quartet had floated between men on stilts and trampled over confetti to arrive at the Eagle's Table.

Descending along a set of stairs from the sidewalk, Pauthor was eye-level with the restaurant's roof. On it, an ornamental table rested on the paws and backs of carved forest creatures, all with strained upward stares. The one theme Pauthor recognized immediately was that the lesser beings were all in various states of misery. The crying turtle clutching a handkerchief of hickory, the squirrel guarding her last acorn, the envious jay and a pair of weasels fighting over a fallen scrap. On the table itself, crowned atop an array of sticks meant to resemble a grand nest, there burned and boiled a massive gold chalice inside a massive golden bowl. While the chalice held a steady flame, the bowl itself boiled with blood that slopped and gurgled down onto the nest and the wooden faces below. Above the menagerie, a giant leering eagle stretched its Padauk wings.

While the top floor of the restaurant was reserved for the House of Ouvarnia, the bottom was in no shortage of decorative robes and studded brooches. Amidst the swirling skirts of serving wenches, over glasses of wine and the quartet's dismembering of oysters, a spirited talk ensued over the rise of the Chapwyn religion in Rehleia.

"Our trades are doomed," the poet called Niovel continued, "all doomed." And to him in his lament it appeared so. No amount of tickles or back slaps pulled him from himself. "The arts will be constricted now, now that the tyrants draped in humility and meekish rags are covering our peninsula."

"Oh, don't fret, Niovel," Tinora said. "Their priests and those Ansul's True soldier types don't have nearly the foothold they boast about in their sermons. Why, just today, in the opium dens, we heard talk of our dear friend Pauthor's quaint homelands." She turned to Pauthor. "Is it true bores from Oxghorde go all the way down to Amden to try and conjure up some ghostly sorcerer from a graveyard?"

"I really don't," Pauthor said, "that is, my father and I don't—"

"He doesn't know," the tiny man said, rattling ringlets once more to run fingers through his hair. "Too busy tilling the brilliant muds and what forth. And they call the 'ghostly sorcerer' *He*, Tinora. Simply *Him*. Tighten your lore and loosen your braids, dear girl."

Though Pauthor heard them, he was able to focus only on his elation. Fen-lung already seemed to be but a memory, turning to vapor. And in a lone night's stumble, he'd landed in a parade of legitimized artisans—souls who knew the true artist had to dedicate oneself to a life of ridicule, even mild banishment. Those who have accepted this, they toil, often in obscurity, pulling the human experience into chosen mediums until, if bled for long enough, hard enough, life grants them the greatest purpose under the stars.

It was only fitting then, the moodiness. Further talk of Chapwyn priests petitioning to have Nettielium painted over women's nipples; those who lived for the freedom of their medium were bound to ponder such somber thoughts from time to time.

A moment's trip to the polished latrines placed the somberness squarely in Pauthor's lap, and purse. At his table were three kicked-over chairs and a bill demanding more money than his father made in a month. The doormen, faces as solemn as the statues they resembled, were the next Pelliulis he'd encounter. From the nearest window, he heard a ruckus that could have come from any departing gaggle, laughing in triumph. "Star-struck one," however—he knew the owner of that squalid mirth.

It wasn't so much the crockery or the mugs, but the dungeon-grade pots and pans that made his cook-overseen servitude so miserably extended. The long-forgotten pans had been waiting for him at the bottom of the tub, so thick with grease and slick he had to pry them apart. Halfway into working off the first batch of Royal Oysters, he staggered out from the kitchen's rear door just in time to vomit.

Not only a fool, but a sick fool. Not only a sick fool, but one who batted away a sensation even more nauseous than the fate awaiting him inside. He knew every thread of the quilt lying on his old bed, yet here, with no sight of even being paroled from the kitchen, there was no bed for him to collapse into. Another payload of his stomach came up, this one signed off to the most unwelcome homesickness in all Mulgara.

"A few more steps and you would have cleared the loading dock," a voice from behind him said. "They left you with the bill, didn't they?"

Pauthor wasn't sure if it was her catlike smile or the casual way she spelled out what was turning out to be the worst night of his life. Choosing a favored verse from Vandahl, he spit: "Empty thy all-seeing crystal ball into my veins," adding short, "why don't you," then lurching forward to exorcise more carrot mush and Rigl.

His longing for home must have knocked something loose. Her laugh sounded like it came from Amden.

Her wench's uniform said she also worked for the Eagle's Table, though by the cocking of her hip, the bounce of her midnight bangs, she at least appeared she did so happily. It was peculiar, familiar: her somewhat wider bones under girlish, tan skin.

"So you work here, then?" she said. "First night?"

"No. I mean—yes—the bill. Never mind." Composing himself, he wiped his hands on his breeches, before finally extending one: "Pauthor, Pauthor Quithot."

"Hortence Rehton."

His senses hadn't fooled him, then. The fates had yet to cease pulling his strings. The mightiest of the minor houses, these potion-makers took to large huts in Amden's swamps. It was a Rehton one would expect to tame the great beasts, concoct some gurgling broth to realign the heavens, and it was the Rehtons, not the House of Lotgard, rumored to have commanded the respect of energumens from the most western dock of Nilghorde to the sandy shores of Azad.

Spare no space for cliché—with her warm handshake came a vial. An energy potion to liven him up for the night's "remaining obligations," she explained.

Upon the cork hitting the cobblestones and the black liquid hitting his lips, the world somehow revealed itself to Pauthor for the very first time.

𝓧

Though intended to be drab by the PCA, the walls in Pauthor's dorm had been inadvertently painted by slings of teal and an entire jar of azure, right alongside canvas after canvas in a roar of productivity.

Drugs were as woven into the fabric of Pelliul's reputation as were the city's aesthetics. That they'd proliferate in its academic halls were a certainty. And in the halls of the Pelliul College of Art—an outright sacrilege if not. Though Pauthor had fumbled into misfortune upon arrival, in the mere span of a month, he had nestled into a lively purpose.

Maybe it was Hortence's own longing for home, that inner whisper calling for the warmth of origin. If this had brought them into each other's arms, being lovers with the hall's prominent drug pusher certainly didn't hurt Pauthor's arrangement, which was becoming as exciting as riding a dragon.

Her bestsellers were those black vials. Tasting like licorice root and burning the nose hairs, her cauldron's main effort brought forth the pit-fighter out of the dullard, the sprite from the slug, the talkative socialite out of the morose maladroit.

Though it didn't surprise Pauthor that Hortence's family had money, it surprised him even less that she would keep with bog traditions and find clever ways to earn a little more. Though her father paid her tuition to pursue theatre, she pocketed what was sent, swished a leather skirt at the Eagle's Table, and erected a witch's chemistry set.

Entering her dorm room, there were days when Pauthor considered holding his breath and donning a soldier's helmet. There were usually an assortment of buyers lining the hall or trailing not far behind him. The occasional set of eyes, nervously blinking out from wrapped scarves, only heightened his suspicion that one day Hortence was going to unleash a noxious flume, eradicating a score of aspiring singers and painters, or blow the place sky high.

Those who made it past the mists beheld frothing racks. Among the pops of amethyst and veiled cages of chirps and rattles sat the arsenal of Hortence's discipline. He'd counted close to fifteen potions once, all separated by color, odor, or a label with crossbones and a grinning skull. One of the larger frothed white, smelling like flowers. Despite its pleasantness to at least one of the senses, dormitory roaches, unconquerable even in this bustling lab, were forever avoiding its bubbles that made it down to the barren floor.

Other potions also sold with regularity. One, made by crushing a live cricket and mixing its remains, the drinker would be taken off by a powerful slumber. A beleaguered student, finally caught up on a cruel syllabus, could be fully restored in no longer than the lifespan of a campfire.

Another was a diluted version of a Rehton trick Pauthor had heard about since boyhood. Used by the Rehton clan to ensure they could harvest on the fringes without fear of being mauled, they'd sprinkle the hallucinogen into the water surrounding plots that held their esoteric bulbs and vine. Any beasts nearby would ingest it and become disoriented, culminating in a confused non-violent menagerie where crocodiles had been seen spinning in the mud, nipping at nothing. Though the energy boosters had quickly become Pauthor's favorite, one or two vials of this dorm-championed psychedelia had inspired a painting that brought him new discoveries every time he gazed upon its glorious confusion.

Wrapped together in Pauthor's cot one evening. "And your mother?" Hortence asked, sidling up against his thigh.

"Left. Took my sister with her."

"To where?"

"Oxghorde, last anyone heard."

"But you stayed."

"I guess I couldn't do it to him. Besides," propping up, taking a mocking tone, "Paulie, *yerr* not gonna abandon me like the rest of the girls, are ya?"

"Poor, poor Amden patriarchs—hey, that sounds like a play."

Her inquiry about what caused the final dissolution of the Quithots invoked the same old story, pulled out like a bottom-drawer garment.

It had been the Party of the Rains. When the frogs provided in cage-top punch bowls had all been squeezed of their powers, Orloc had snuck away. Right before the crowning of the mud prince and mud princess, he came careening through in howl-ing revelry, passing out on the toes of a local authority figure. Pauthor's mother retraced her husband's steps, finding the stash he'd smuggled, dead as doornails and in the same supine X as her snoring embarrassment.

"Right. In its last moments," Hortence said, tracing his nipple, "the glower flashes and blasts its killer with fantastic joy."

Pauthor guzzled another energy vial. Some empties were broken on the floor, but they were soon forgotten when the liquid conjoined he and his lover once more.

)X(

For all the ruckus of lovemaking and drug use—two conventions Pauthor had always ascribed as necessary for receiving artistic revelations—nothing helped his mood as he skulked toward the office of Professor Majot.

"Scribblers," Pauthor mumbled, shouldering past the usual clog of students and climbing the marble steps. It was widely known that Majot was the preeminent authority in putting one's observations to line. The drawing professor had helped renovate mansions and done the illustrations for the *Transient State of Grace* comeback edition. It was only fitting, then, that Pauthor's appallingly low marks came with a suggestion that he drop everything and consult a man for whom sketches tossed in a wastebasket ended up covering the decorative armor of the Ward's highest echelon.

No closed doors for genius—upon weaving through towers of brightly bound books, Pauthor made his way to concave alternations of marble and glass. Though the college was only halfway up one of the city's three great summits, from the windows a gazer could easily take in Pelliul's sparkling vastness.

Where a tourist may have sat and peered through a telescope, a giant stand bore the backside of a canvas. Majot's bare feet moved with his chuckles and whistles. Pauthor cursed as he tried to maintain a swaying book tower he'd fumbled against.

"Dance lessons are six doors down," Professor Majot said.

With the books now calmed, Pauthor could turn his attention to this face that had popped out from behind the canvas. He'd heard Majot was young, but by all the gods who bestow, this prodigy could be no more than thirty.

"Professor—"

"Insolent beanstalk," the professor snapped. "Disturb my work, and not even for the right reasons. Dancers. You dance well?"

"No. Sir, I—" up-righting himself, "I'm a painter...or at least one day hope to be."

This brought Professor Majot out and into full view. Swinging a brush, the very essence of artistic royalty neared. Leaning into Pauthor's ear, "We either are, or are not, dearest amphibian."

"Professor."

"That's Lord Professor."

"Lord—"

"Tersiona's sweet ass, man!" Majot exploded in mirth. Pauthor had fallen back against the stack that now rained down on him. Amidst the flittering pages he saw Majot's smile. "Majot is out sick. Lordy, you would of throated me like an addict if I'd just wiggled out the tip." Pulling Pauthor to his feet, "They call me Vernónn." His smile white as demons.

After a tour of the office, including a one-sided discussion on the entanglement of cartoonish genitalia currently being painted, Professor Majot's student assistant, Vernónn Ouvarnia, handed Pauthor the appropriate manuals.

There was no need to return. In just a few weeks, mutating in sense and memory as shorter or long in certain spaces, it was as if Pauthor had been tutored by Majot himself. It turned out his newest encounter wasn't just a raving lunatic, a lover of elderberry, and a sworder, but an emerging artistic heavyweight in his own right.

Though as instant as spring lightning, and as off-kilter as befriending a court jester and a hyena at the same time, friends they became. Pauthor, though hating stereotypes in art, relished finding them in life. *Come to Pelliul to snuggle with mighty folk*, the saying goes; made love to by a Rehton then claimed by an Ouvarnia.

Despite owning gilded swords worth more than entire Amden plantations, the young aristocrat enjoyed the "vulgar bliss" of lower classes. This put Vernónn down into freshman dorms on most days already, and now that he'd assigned himself as Pauthor's tutor, his explosive wayfaring often flopped him into Pauthor's room and company.

)X(

In this blur, two years were born and died.

)X(

"Take but a bit, my Paulie," Hortence said, "A little—that's okay, but it advances aging if overdone." They were in her room; her putting on the last bit of fashionable ensemble, he waiting, seated on the edge of her cot.

Pauthor didn't know what irked him more. By the time his junior year had arrived, and senior coronations had ceremonied over the heads of Hortence and Vernónn, he'd felt the warm embrace of self-worth. Along with this came a heightened dislike for snide remarks. Even when attending one of Hortence's many plays, on most nights he insisted on decorating himself with a sharp sword. One whose purchase, after receiving the highest marks in a favored class, almost sent him to the poor house. He had found self-worth, he declared, not brashness, and with such treasure came little interest in suffering even the slightest condescension.

These were new days. Fen-lung was gone. Without having to breathe through what felt like a dampened sock, his work's heroic figures no longer held an assertion totally unknowable to their creator. To be ostracized for drinking energy potions was all the more ludicrous being her number-one client. So what if he'd stolen one or two? She'd left them out, and an artist's mind is not just self-aware, but aware of the pushes and pulls inside of others. Expecting that it was her worrisome way of being nice, or her nice way of being worrisome, leaving them out for him was worth what came after.

Her preaching was only rivaled in its irksomeness by calling him that oafish "Paulie." After a moment, he resumed reading the scroll in his hands:

Dearest Pauthor Quithot,

Greetings from our fair fens and bowers. It is with no pleasure that I write. Orloc died. As you wellest know our protocol and our ways, being denizen temporarily removed, since no heir was present to claim rights during or after his burial, we are selling all properties but your primary parcels. Out-of-towners want them, Tersiona knows why.

Your esteemed Commissioner,

Murgle Qell

Hortence had learned, sometimes suffered, much during their pillow talks. These were the times Pauthor strived for intimacy. She learned just as much when he didn't.

On good days, he'd rival Vernónn for vivacity of the student bathhouse or the entertainment in the bleachers of the fighting pits between manglings. On bad days, he was a corpse, shivering only to muse how he'd never touch a brush again.

News of his father's death left her on pins and needles. It was harder for Pauthor to hate someone who was now gone. Far worse than losing one we adore, the longing, the futile hope to move the stars to their correct position, this noble futility that motivates wayward soldiers and stalwart starving poets had now left. Now, only the ghosts and he to dance among them—wondering over what to feel and what might have been.

Hortence's strategizing how best to gauge his mood was halted when he sat up and said, "Vernónn says tonight'll be crazier than our last few, if you can believe that."

Vernónn was right.

Ж

Pelliul had a reputation for all sorts of fun conventions involving two men and a woman. Less lascivious than the fabled introductions at the Pulsing Plum Baths, but the three had formed their own parade of wildness and thrills. It was Vernónn's lock-picking kit that had got them into situations as exhilarating as they were illegal—two things Vernónn always claimed could not exist without the other.

The Eagle's Table was not a one-time site for Pauthor. Needing money far more than Vernónn, and having far fewer ways to earn it than Hortence, he had transitioned after the first encounter to wiping glasses and banging pots for a wage. It was also not a one-time occurrence that Vernónn would be sat amongst his kinsmen while Hortence brought out roasted geese on bronze pikes and Pauthor later relieved the pikes of their residue.

The lavishness of Ouvarnian flare trickled down even to their tribe's art scholar's mischief. Pauthor couldn't help but be reminded he was a waterlogged farm boy whenever Vernónn summoned a particular pick or key from his kit. The small box was made entirely of ornate stained glass. When those golden hinges opened, sneaking around galleries the night before grand openings became a favorite indulgence. But like with all indulgences, before long came the need to supersede it.

It was perhaps the fancy kit's coffin shape that had sparked the hair on Pauthor's back when two chittering picks granted them entrance into the crocodile pits after hours.

Amid a battle with stubborn pieces of rice between fork tines, recounting that night's luridness to himself made Pauthor tarry between chuckling and succumbing to a cold sweat. He'd dodged at least one swinging tail, but the unreliability of a torchless moon instilled nightmares that he'd dodged even worse. His hands needing relief from the soap and his back from the bending, the loading dock welcomed him as he exited the rear door and sat on its slope.

No sooner had he sat down then he began to hear approaching voices.

"And the carved menagerie," a man said. "You must see it around front here."

"Really? Niovel, you are King Meticulous of the Dandys."

Before he'd fully grasped his encounter, Pauthor found he'd come to his feet and was standing just a pot's throw from the sneak-thieving pageant who'd led him here his first night in the city. The softer side of him, the part of him which he'd grown to despise, clung to a hope they'd moved on to better endeavors. But their fourth figure in tow, looking as lost and as vexed and as spellbound as he'd once been, only confirmed the Eagle's Table was a feasting ground for more than Vernónn's family.

"The oysters are joyous tonight," Pauthor said, stopping that whore they called Tinora where she strutted.

After a long moment, Niovel spoke. "Thank you, dearest pan-scrub."

Pauthor leapt off the loading dock. Though his fists were balled, any foolish attack he may have carried forth was halted. Hearkening to a whisper and a caress from Tinora, the trio's rube pulled a blade from his breeches.

Pauthor was driven back by its shine. His buttocks met the loading dock, nearly toppling him over. It was as if he were now frozen to that stone, his heart pounding. He knew he was to be sliced to ribbons. Though a country boy dunce, his opponent menaced forward, footstep by footstep, while Tinora yelled what body parts to lop off, and in what order.

A pathetic scream came out of him, but it jettisoned him blindly into a windmill.

He'd heard tales of survivors who'd remembered the slaps of water against their canoe, the taste of that water when having been dragged under by an unsuccessful croc. The senses were funny, especially in times a few collectively perceived death. Though his eyes were clamped shut, he now heard clearly drunken revelry, flutes, something shattering, and the bark of a nearby dog.

When he opened his eyes, his enemy had retreated, faces all frozen in outright fear.

"Eunuchs! Ear Fuckers!" Pauthor lurched forward, picking up the long blade that had been abandoned. The nervousness they wore seemed almost too severe, though he had other matters to concern over now.

A deep growl pulled Pauthor's attention over his shoulder. A large dog with its hackles up stood where the ramp of the loading dock met the alley. He'd first thought it somehow a hallucination, but it wasn't. The dog was really there.

Then Pauthor saw.

Hortence was on the back stairs, holding her hands in the shape of...of a dog's mouth? Odder still—odder than her fingers like fangs, odder than the menacing dog that had begun to slink away, odder than the three con artists who'd already vanished and the back of their would-be-latest mark hurrying in another direction—was that between Hortence and where his miraculous protector had snarled lay not pieces of a broken bottle, as he'd thought he'd heard, but shattered pieces of porcelain.

Hortence beat him to words. "Yes, it's that earring box you gave me. Never really liked it. Sorry, Paulie."

The weeks that followed what Pauthor referred to as the "dog night," his admiration for and consumption of his girlfriend's trickery blossomed to obsession.

"You could clear out a bar with one of these," he said. "Put down the baddest brawler." He was looking at another box, this time not expensive porcelain but a horrid orange, one Hortence had procured from a freshmen claysmith.

"Give it here," Hortence said, then smashed it on her floor. "You load the spell into a receptacle. I don't prefer vials, as they tend not to break and roll around the floor. Break the receptacle to unleash the spell. I hope you're taking notes—I won't repeat it forever, not that a raccoon is going to help you paint. Gnaw down a Rigl stalk, maybe."

Hortence pulled a rat from its cage. In a trance, the rodent mimicked her movements.

"So you preload the command for the animal?"

"One command. Defend. Mimic. Kill," she said, bending and straightening as the rodent did. "One command per receptacle."

"How does the beast know?"

"As you say, you preload it." Hortence grabbed another clay box, this one a less ghastly shade of green. The rat tittered on its hind legs and stuck out a forepaw where its own tiny green box may have been. "Offer itself as food. Serve as a vehicle, if the animal you mean to summon is large enough."

"And only one animal per spell?"

She broke the green one. "Go open that birdcage, please."

A shrill blur of yellow and blue flew out and pecked Pauthor's face as if he were a fox nearing an egg-filled nest. Hortence and her rat danced merrily as Pauthor wrestled the Glaeyling back into its cage.

Over the screeches and rattles, he shouted; "So as long as the animals nearby, you summon it and it does whatever command you loaded?"

"You are indeed the intellectual jewel of our fens, my lover."

⟡

That night no animals were summoned, though Pauthor wished they had been. Vernónn snuck them into a banquet for mercenaries. Employed by the Pelliul Ordrids, getting wined and fattened before some abduction or slaughter, the hung banner of that wicked house was only fair warning. Picking locks got the three of them robbed, or close to it. Sheathing one vile skill to unsheathe another, Vernónn, showing his gleeful familiarity with the pierce and parry, slayed one thug and removed the flail-bearing hand of another.

Worse than not having a potion to gulp or a porcelain container to break was the way Hortence looked at Vernónn after. Then, his blade still dripping, Vernónn's mad, cunning gaze that had returned it.

⟡

Pauthor's newest painting was a flight of untethered golden stairs, lofting on the wind up to meet the heavens. The Crocodiles Night, the Dog Night, and the Night Eyes Met That Shouldn't, he himself had climbed such a rickety path and now hung in pessimism.

His and Hortence's lovemaking remained much the same, although he found new and creative ways to vent his frustration. He just hoped that it all had restated his love for, and yes, he dared proclaim, his right to say that such a woman was his.

Ponies as a boy and lavish praise for feats in his medium were not enough for the dashing Vernónn Ouvarnia.

As predictable as the first drop that commences the Party of the Rains, one night Pauthor found Vernónn in Hortence's room. Though both were clothed. Vernónn stood while Hortence sat on the edge of her bed. The worry in her eyes said all her mouth didn't.

In his family's official regalia, Vernónn's black leather shined and creaked. "Evening, Paulie."

"All the rent and gash and gigglin' girls. Tersiona's mottled cunt! Every goldcoin-sucker without a care or ankles that've ever met, and you have to go for her?"

Pauthor couldn't recall all the insults and accusations that followed, the trits about mushroom farmers and unsteady hands. All he remembered was walking to Hortence's frothing rack, chugging an energy potion, then drawing his sword.

"Don't be foolish," Vernónn said, whose snobbery was at its worst when stepping into a tierce, as he now did, pointing that thin, shiny blade at Pauthor's heart.

Hortence shot to her feet and was between them. It was no learned rapier that tore through Pauthor's chest. She moved closer, but to Vernónn.

Pauthor felt himself vanishing, as if what was left of him was a mere wisping shadow of what pounded and shook and pleaded a moment before. He could not recall a single worthy deed he had ever done. Eager for friends was normal, expected even, especially for a stranger in a looming boisterous city who'd lived his days amongst the slitherers and squirrels of a bog. He couldn't be blamed for tramping around with such villainy, though with all his soul he wanted to. His dead dad on a frog night would have maybe called it "shattered," and only this shattering was stronger than the potion in his veins. He dropped his sword.

"I would skin any woman alive," Pauthor said, unable to look at that whore, "smack down their twitchin' remains and tan their hides just so she could avoid mud on her heels." To him it sounded like a roar, but he knew it wasn't. She refused to look up from the floor. Pauthor hung his head.

"Compelling, Pauthor, really," Vernónn said, sliding his free

arm over Hortence's shoulder and turning for the door. "Make a
masterpiece of it one day."

)(

The rotting town of Amden had served the Municipal One in
two ways. Soldier food had been provided, and much of the real
estate unused for mushroom farming was deemed suitable for the
casualties of the wars.

Once the bloodbaths in Azad and domestic battles with resil-
ient Ordrids commenced, corpses impaled, infiltrated by diseases
or decay, or all three arrived to Amden in droves. By the time the
Years of Peace trumpeted in distant streets, the graveyard at the
town's outskirts had swollen to resemble a sinking city. But though
it was a perfect dumping ground for injured crocodile hunters who
couldn't pay back those who'd lent them money for their spears,
many boglings still buried their dead on family ground.

Dropping out of the Pelliul School of Art was easy; slumping
back home was not.

Like everything, the Quithot graves clustered on the edge of
the swamp. A few still held their white amongst all the crooked
headstones losing protracted battles with lichen. The newest addi-
tion, white as Majot's office marble, held Orloc's name.

"Sorry I couldn't," Pauthor muttered, being pulled away for
the second time by a passing calamity of bells and stench.

"Sorry, I couldn't—will you get your damn lummoxin' cows
off my land!"

The Pelat chirped. Pauthor reckoned it was better he didn't
hear what the herdsmen had replied. He withdrew his hand from
the headstone. That commissioner hadn't missed a thing.

Pelats had started their free migration into Rehleia years ago,
taking their shrunken-head necklaces and skinny cows to places
like Amden, on land that had formerly been his family's. Now
they were in Pauthor's lap.

Reassuming the family business was as formidable in its misery as the immediate return of fen-lung. Though it helped him at times forget about his uncouth neighbors, lethargy took hold of him with new resolve. No access to energy potions worsened his rib-rattling malaise.

Coughing, he freed a crate from webs and dust to resume his painting. His work at first inward and wild, they were not for therapy nor joy, but to barter with the Rehtons for deluded versions of Hortence's old broth.

This proved harder than he had hoped. He came to find out that Orloc had burned many bridges, making trade with anyone unusually difficult and often demeaning. Negotiations improved when he started painting celebrations of Rehton matriarchs: curvy, steely-eyed women, caressing lounging lizards. Only he recognized the innuendos and sly digs. Trade became even better when he began painting tortured Ouvarnias for the Qells. But in the too-often draughts of exchange or inspiration, Pauthor resorted to things he would never have admitted to anyone, even if there had been a willing ear.

The heavy rains would begin soon, and with the weather wouldn't just come the excited chorus lights and *ribbits* of the shallows, but also the paw prints in the mud: monsters out of deep water. This season, while he managed a paltry patch of Rigl, Pauthor considered those coming paw prints, and that maybe he'd dawdle near the deeper pools at sundown.

To combat such despairs, Pauthor occupied his mind with attempts at replicating that bitch's *Beast Summoner* potion. The ingredients were abundant in the bog. The words he remembered. A caged rat of his own and failures enumerable left every combination of the words uttered, every empty jar broken and strewn about the floor. Until, at last, one day his rodent rose to its hind legs and mimicked his sour jubilation.

Pauthor pulled out a glass bottle Orloc had stored hooch in

when the frogs evaded him for painful stretches. The cork was still good.

He could hear the Pelat's cows. When not clinking their irksome bells, they would liberate themselves from corrals of sticks and trample his Rigl patch. They smelt worse than the swamp would to a foreigner who didn't shrink heads. Worst yet was their master's primitive approach of burning shit to make bricks for some other unsightly hovel. Pauthor was no murderer. The Pelats were safe. His neighbor's bevy of swamp cattle, however, might be dragged to the murky depths. Considering the paw prints once more and hoping to marvel at the carnage from the distance of his porch, "Kill all in front of me" was Pauthor's command. He loaded the corked bottle accordingly.

A month into the storms, just as his isolation was beginning to thicken, the visitors came. Articulate eruptions from the pools, what he thought were knocks on the front door or claws at the rear, all causing Pauthor to peer from the window, straining out into emptiness. The candles he held would sometimes show faces in the swelling puddles, on the evening leaves, or in the fat drops of rain that seemed to hover. Then there was nothing. No one.

One night the storms bore him a rain-drenched woman.

"Pauthor," Hortence quivered.

"No marsh mansion," Pauthor said, watching her gaze up into the rafters and down at all the clutter. After a while: "Why are you here?"

"Here." She held out a shiny black vial.

"Peace offering," Pauthor scoffed, shutting and locking the door behind her. "Buy me off with the old fix? Come home to enchant fish with Uncle Boraor for a holiday and find time to slump and sate guilt? Don't sit there. In fact, don't sit anywhere." He snatched the vial, tossing its cork. "Guilt, you know nothin' of."

"Paulie."

"Don't call me that. The Rehton is the swarmer of flies—"

"Pauthor."

"The enchantress who flows through the throat to be captor of the brain."

"I'm pregnant."

"The…" He felt as if the air had been sucked from the room. He emptied the vial into his guts.

"Yeah."

"And what of it!?" He was in the air. "Amazing! Blessed are the stars! The conjoinin' of two famed Houses." He relished the tightening of her full lips, the hurt furrow of her brow. "Your spawn'll have a snake's belly."

With synthetic energy pumping, only making him hate her more, he let loose profanity to shake the heavens. As he was pulling her over to his latest project, an Ouvarnia being trampled by a horse, she stopped him.

Pressed against her kiss, he didn't know where or what he was. All at once, hate and what some called love intertwined and took one another to a swirling bed.

)(

"I had no choice but to go with him," she said, rolling onto the moist spot. "He marched in that day, demanding I be his. He doesn't understand the meaning of the word no—and, I'm sorry, he would have killed you in that foolish little duel. I snuck away as soon as I could."

Pauthor's triumphant joke that he'd brutalized his manhood against the gooey, Ouvarnian clump inside of her had prompted this diatribe.

"He's become even more obsessive and deranged," she was saying.

Pauthor's eyes widened as she made sense of years of untethered madness. For all the swashbuckling and tarts on the arm, the great Vernónn Ouvarnia was as limp as a swamp-weed.

"—waiting to sneak away with no worry he'd follow, so yes, I had to go with him, Paulie."

Sunk in devilish glee, he could only replay humiliating visions of Vernónn chastising his clutched member in front of school-girls barely able to hide their giggles. Certainly Hortence could have whipped up some potion for that? And…why hadn't she just poisoned him the first week and then skipped to Amden with a minstrel train?

None of these questions were asked, for nothing less terrible than a monsoon of sabers, no question nor fantasy nor horror could have moved him more than Hortence confirming whose baby grew inside her.

"A sleep potion," Pauthor almost thought he had said. "Really, *whore*tence, though your skills at theatre are as shameful as this *town*," said a voice Pauthor couldn't believe he was hearing, "I'd at least hoped for some originality in your treachery."

Vernónn was at the front door, swollen and reddened and wreaking. He tossed his lock-picking kit to the floor. In his other hand was his rapier.

There is a fable, one about a proud falcon who once found a mirror. Carrying it back to its nest, the falcon groomed itself to the envy of all other birds. But when a passing owl pointed out a missing feather on the back of the falcon's head, the falcon killed every creature it could before diving into the glass.

Vernónn sneered. Hortence screamed as he charged the bed.

Pauthor scrambled to his worktable, where he seized his father's old hooch bottle. Fear had stricken him as if a monster from the swamp had shouldered into his home. He broke the bottle against the wall. His eyes were on the open door.

Vernónn's perplexed laughter, wicked and foul, rang off the pitiful little paint jars, the rafters, out into pouring rain.

"Royalty before peasantry, mother always said." Vernónn said, crawling on the bed and then standing tall.

Pinned by a boot, Hortence swung her eyes on Pauthor. She was to be run through, and he was to stop it. He saw the long blade, angled down, ready. He saw the girl who'd spared him a similar doom, now two lives, not one. And he saw the fiend he could not beat, but yet the fiend he would have to. More hate and panic ever thought capable in a man finally lit Pauthor on fire. Grabbing his sickle and darting to certain death, he was knocked flat by a crocodilian monster that careened through the door, bursting the frame like splinters, and snapped Vernónn in two.

Screams and explosions of hot blood nailed Pauthor to the floor. Thrumming growls, moans out of primeval muck, it gnawed on still-squirming bones. It was all he could hear.

The beast stopped with the remaining heap and creaked its neck toward Pauthor. Frozen, he only found a frantic scream when those yellow watery eyes turned to Hortence. For the second time, she shot a look at him that would make him dance on the moon or dig to Hell. The beast could swallow a meal whole, he'd learn. This stare was different, and she held it, terrible and hateful and fierce, even as a long tongue wrapped around her legs.

)(

When it was done, Pauthor and the beast stared at each other. The *Beast Summoner* had worked, to the letter. Stuck somewhere between the purest of fears and wishing that he were next, he watched as it licked where its lips would have been, and then dragged itself back out into the night.

Pauthor stood at the mirror and noted the ribbons of his hair, grayed not just because of great fear. How he had withered himself.

He pulled out his easel and wept until his eyes were matted in filth. His door was mangled. Outside its yawning blackness, a cowbell donged in the Rigl patch.

Pauthor put away his brushes. All that was left of Vernónn

was his stained-glass box; all intact, save for a pick jammed in the flattened door lock.

"Should break easy enough," Pauthor said, picking up the kit. Working in seclusion would engulf him, but first he needed to summon more monsters. They needed to learn the whereabouts of a few cows.

AMDEN BOG

A jaw a be a snappin',
Another thing a happen,
Comin' somethin' else,
Be better not a nappin'.
'Cause Mulgara be a dark one,
Our water loves to stir,
One and two, a wizard's brew,
You be callin' somethin' 'sir.'

— *Diddy of the Wary Bogling Trotliner*

I

A CULTIST'S RETURN

Time has a way of seeping by in the bog. The day's errands are met and at night put away with the fishing tackle and the scythe. Storms come and go, as do creatures, eating one moment, eaten the next. Trees, giants, hurl themselves into black water to be ignited by spore and fern, bursting through dying trunks, reaching for their own pieces in the sky. In this green wheel Pauthor lived and toiled and he moldered, and Matina, who became primeval royalty, actualized and retrograded accordingly.

※

Two long years. Two long years passed after a Gorsuka had been killed during the Party of the Rains, and two long years passed before Ledgor stepped foot in Amden again. Upon his priestess Niesuri's death, her father—that political rot-grub—exhausted the town treasury, employing able-backed thugs who turned over every canoe and skewered every soggy bale.

Ledgor's beloved Order had quickly dwindled to nothing when Commissioner Qell discovered the "cult paraphernalia" in Priestess Niesuri's chambers, after discovering the blood and hair and gore in that Matina girl's hut the night prior. Impaled on stakes, only one of the six was a member of the Order, but even one gave Qell's thugs enough information to scatter them to the winds.

Like that Matina bitch, Ledgor had only one name. This was just fine by him. It would be easier for them to remember. It would soon be hissed and spoke in trembling whispers by the swamp's fetid denizens for decades to come, until the river finally swallowed them and shat them out into the indifference of the sea.

His love for the majestic Gorsuka paled next to his love for the late priestess. Both loves had only intensified as he'd slogged away in an Oxghorde lumber yard, unfriendly and barren as his boarding house. Longed he did: for his priestess's soft hand, for the shimmer of the waters once more, and for its finest and noblest beasts to rise one day and crush those who walked on two legs.

With the Order gone, Ledgor's mind—a mind once ridiculed by his grim grandmother as "simple"—had melded his two great passions. And now he was back. Just as a swift kick and a passing crocodile simultaneously launched his matriarch and began his tumultuous freedom, invoking Niesuri's ghost would bind her to him. The witch in Oxghorde had said so.

Once privy to Niesuri's secrets, a mighty Gorsuka would be in his power. How his fantasies oscillated—from riding one's back through the parting waters, to commanding savage jaws through parting crowds. Amden would see a pale rider, hair blacker than pitch and wetter than rain, wreaking absolute and final havoc on those who'd shunned him.

Rising to his feet, cinching the hood of his sacred Gorsukan Order cloak, Ledgor cursed at and kicked the bevel marker that had tripped him in the graveyard. Catching the marble corner with a toe had sent him dancing, muffling his howl in his hand. Hopping on his good foot, he read as best he could the letters, knowing then whose name he spat on.

Crowns of gravestones and a hulking, sinking columbarium passed as he walked on. Being away from the bog had cleared his nose of many of the smells now refamiliarizing themselves as he breathed. The flitter of bugs who's mating dusts coated his cloak. The moist air, that mix of reptilian breath and summer showers. And that moldering decay under forever-bursting life.

As advised, the spell could only be performed during a moonless night. A torch or lantern was out of the question. Last thing Ledgor needed was getting picked up right before arriving at Niesuri's. He did have light waiting; a tallow candle, as lone as he was. The thought of what he'd do if it wouldn't light enraged him further as he toppled over a half-sunken sarcophagus.

Now it was known amongst the Order, Niesuri's preference for other women. This disappointing perversion of nature, however, hadn't stopped Ledgor from committing theft during one of the group's late-night swims. But the jewel of his infatuation, she certainly observed the fullness of uninterrupted nature in other, equally inconvenient ways. Meant to sate his urges, the discovery of how soiled the priestesses' undergarments were ruined him beyond all hope. Flashes of gushing blood or clumps of human debris infiltrated his fantasies, all from the female ebb and flow, as foreign to his experience as was disgusting to his tastes.

The witch had told him how fortunate he'd been for not parting with Niesuri's undergarments. Extracted from the cloth, a mere drop of Niesuri's blood had been mixed with his own, then penned to parchment.

As Ledgor approached the Qell family mausoleum, he recounted the process. The old hag had taken his lumber yard wages in exchange for the scroll he was now unrolling, and a directive he'd surely remembered: "On the new moon, and on the grounds in which the world knows her grave."

When the candle wick lit, it was as if the flint possessed a crack of thunder. To his luck, nobody patrolled these graves. One side of this damn waste of real estate served as hoot-and-belch-filled housing for those yet to be housed in that columbarium. But he was a wanted man. His name and likeness had purportedly been nailed to dock posts and cypress trees as far out as the Pelat herding plots.

Reasonably certain he was alone, he held the candle to the scroll.

He'd gone over the words a hundred times. Went over them in the cramped dankness of the boarding house and in the back of the whiskey-barrel wagon he'd stowed himself in as it bobbed and clacked to join the convoys profitably filling the void in Amden, now that most the glowers were reportedly gone.

Once, after a few beers, Ledgor had read the words off the scroll aloud. His closet door had creaked open to release a ball of dust that amassed to a dancing menace. Though he extinguished this conjuring by frightened stamps and a borrowed broom, he made a point to never repeat this mistake.

His own voice now sounded like a growl to his ears. Taking it one blood-scabbed stanza at a time, each one done became its own victory.

If nothing happened, what would he do then? Shaman Rehton was never in the Order. To the gods and raped by a snake—they'd tried, the hints and anonymous fliers, but the statesmen was disappointingly content with warding off locust plagues and helping fishermen predict the next school runs.

Surely Niesuri, or the ghost of Niesuri, was the only one who knew the exact secrets to summon Gorsuka. He'd seen her do it. Embarrassed, he'd toppled into the canoe over it.

The stars popped a uniformed, momentary glitter. Bearing down on the words, he steadied his scroll hand. The candle wick turned a Bobilulla blue.

He spoke the final word.

Nothing.

He hurled the damned candle into a picket line of graves. Maybe he'd used up all the scroll's power by accident back in Oxghorde? No, a two-bit huckster who peddled charms and spooky-dos had taken his money, and him, aptly, for a fool. Turning to kick another grave, he foamed with visions of running all the way back to Oxghorde to smash that crone.

Then a young woman clad in moonlight whirled out of nowhere to send him sprawling.

)(

"Blood," an incredibly familiar voice said. Ledgor rose to the grey pallor of a graveyard moments before morning.

His blood—their blood—it had brought her back! He muttered as much before he was silenced.

"No," Niesuri spoke, dressed as she'd been the last time he'd seen her alive. Her form moved. The headstone behind her was readable, as if behind a veil of diluted milk. "No, on your head…" She paused.

"Ledgor," he said, putting a hand to his forehead and drawing back fingers messed by clots of blood and blades of grass.

"Led-gor." She followed his rise, watching curiously, repeating his name as he kicked and cursed another bevel marker.

"It's really you," whirling around to meet her stillness with his frantic joy. "It worked."

"How can I help you?"

"Priestess Nie—"

"Priestess?"

"You were head of our Order."

"…How can I help you?"

Ledgor unveiled his plan: to call upon a mighty Gorsuka and avenge their mistreated Order. For the best anyone could gauge a face that had been on the other side of the grave, she seemed attentive enough.

As birds tuned the beginnings of their morning choir, he hit on the final details. But Niesuri worried him, for not only was she fading to hardly a wisp, she kept looking over her shoulder, toward the edge of the graveyard. More than just looking to where graves were being steadily swallowed by the swamp, she was being pulled that way, as if by slight breezes Ledgor was unable to feel. "Come," she interrupted.

As her form diminished, her speed increased, or so Ledgor thought, working himself into a sweat to chase after her. Keeping her within eyesight was a challenge, one that was rewarded with a sudden, waist-deep halt in stagnant greenness.

"There."

What, he thought, batting away the morning's first Winged Scourge, *a thicket of vine and muck?* Something rubbed against his leg, making him shiver. As he leered into the yawning jungle, the outline of a doorless, moss-conquered mausoleum began to take shape.

Niesuri spoke, "Calling scaled beasts, as you desire, I am afraid I know no longer. But *He* does."

"*He?*" Squinting at the mausoleum.

"*He* knows many rites. But first *He* must be summoned. Blood of the living to soak in his urn. On a new moon, the rites must be spoken."

Ledgor pulled himself out of the swamp. *Urn?* His heart boomed with a terrible worry that he should have been writing all of this down.

As if reading his mind, "I know the rites to summon *Him,*" said only a floating smile.

"How? If you can't—"

"There are other gifts that await us beyond the grave. I'll say them to you. We can call *Him* forward, next moonless night."

"No moon for this next one too?"

"It's sort of a rule," Niesuri said, formless but near, with a tone that reminded him of her old giggle.

Standing in soggy boots and the burgeoning sun, he felt he had to. "Priestess, if someone did somethin' to you, that Matina girl or someone else, lemme know and I'll kill 'em. Just..." His voice had that squeak that used to drive his grandmother to force his hand in boiling water, the squeak when he doubted himself. "How did you die?"

Snakes were descending the canopies, while drunkards waking in the graveyard's far end howled their morning crudeness. "I don't remember," she said, then he was alone once more.

𝕏

Ledgor had once cut Rigl. However, after stacking mushroom heads the size of shields, he had humbled himself beyond the slope of even the lowest Amden commoner.

Working for a Pelat was like cleaning a slave's shit pit. The tiny people's recent emancipation wasn't forgotten in that colloquial analogy. It wasn't the cacophony of their cow bells that drove him partly mad, nor their chirps that passed as language, but the reaction of the town after a long day cleaning Pelati pig pens. It was like he'd defiled some Honor of the People, slopping pig shit atop the monolith every time a coin was let go from brown, spidery hands. In this way, Ledgor had found something kindred in the Pelats. Ducking under the low frame of the old pen, he made a promise to himself that he'd spare most of them when his plan took effect.

"Ah, Letgor," said the old man, emptying a bucket of slop into a trough. Deforesting the swamp to feed their imported stock was one of the few xenophobic criticisms the town had been able to hold onto. An array of snorting heads jockeyed for position as the tattooed, hairless monkey greeted him with a filthy hand.

Niesuri had explained before whisking off that, down the stairs of the moss-eaten mausoleum, an urn awaited. Once filled with blood, some apparition called *He*, or *Him*, was apparently ready to hop out and tell all the world's secrets.

Ledgor needed a pig, and beyond his rapport with Mr. Metek, a Pelat pig was the cheapest.

"Yes, yass, get you good piglet," Mr. Metek said, holding up a squealer. "No? Bigger? Here, what 'bout this big strong girl?"

"Oxghorde. Back now, for a little while anyhow." Ledgor talked to the grey ponytail that whipped and waved behind the sow. When Pelats open up to you, they do so like a thunderstorm. Ledgor answered questions that had been rattled off at him as they'd made their way past the gilts. "I just need to know the best way to bleed one."

"I bleed it here for you." Mr. Metek masterfully flipped a boning knife into the air, "free of charge."

"Need to fatten 'er first."

"Ah, big feast? Sure, sure. Very well. Coins now?"

Ledgor helped with a noose around a gilt's rear legs. Hoisted in the air, the Pelat tied off the rope and brained the pig with a hammer.

"First, stun them. After, slit throat." The Pelat stuck his knife into the neck, moving the blade until it was met with a surge. "You want this," he dipped his free hand into the bright red blood. "Meat will be clean."

"Mr. Metek, how exactly did you get into butcherin'?" Ledgor already knew, but the answer always had a way of galvanizing him.

"You mean after the Conqueror raped my lands and peoples and I needed job? Easy, Letgor: money. But, before that *Missipal One* made us lay our blades in our own sand, we hung from the palms many SS horse boys." The Pelat brought Ledgor his sow and handed over the rat-eaten rope that would serve as a leash. "Like I say," his wink washed back his years, "meat will be clean."

ж

"Be gone, wizardin' scum!" The man roared, kicking at Ledgor's breeches. The burly bootlegger had gladly rented Ledgor his second hut—more an abandoned project than an intended source of income.

That rabble of planks that had been pried from docks and the sawgrass laid on them to rot had served Ledgor well enough in the last month. He'd been able to dodge the rains enough to avoid illness, the snakes enough to avoid heart-stopping agony, and by surviving off swamp cabbage, he'd nourished his bones and fattened his most important sow.

He couldn't stay with Mr. Metek. One of the Pelat's wives had always hated Ledgor, bent on a near-constant accusation that he was practicing black magic. "Sorry, Letgor," was the last Ledgor had heard, coming from the doorway and blocking a clucking harem that had been set on high.

To avoid being identified, the outskirts was the next best thing.

"Your whiskey's worse than piss!" Ledgor yelled back, making his retreat. He'd never tasted the bootlegger's broth and was now burdened under the weight of a pig. He would have to come back to tell that cocksucker a better one, this time with a finer animal, and on top of it. Ledgor's mood brightened, however, as he realized he was about to live up to that Pelati woman's nightmares.

This clump of land he was leaving was so out on the fringes, as long as he didn't tamper with the distiller or let his pig gorge on any Rigl, the last of his copper could pay his rent. Only certain men had commissioner-signed permits to sell booze, and his recently former landlord wasn't one of them. Figuring Ledgor as on the lam for his own reasons, another set of eyes and ears only guarded his work the better.

The bootlegger, whose curses still boomed in the distance, had first loved the arrangement. That was until Niesuri had shown up.

The first night, a hung pot fell, flaming logs rattled in the hearth, and the hut's door swung wide despite the bootlegger swearing he'd locked it.

The second night, last night, Ledgor had been suffocating in the humidity of his hut. Seating himself at its doorless entry, he watched a paler patch of moonlight detach from the trees.

The exchanges between him and his dead priestess's ghost had struck him later as remarkably odd. That it had happened, yes, but also how he'd seemed capable of treating such an extreme event as almost casual. In the weeks that had passed, he'd told himself it was important to remain as steel-nerved come their next encounter. For reasons of personal pride, to say nothing of summoning somethin' that only went by "*He*." As it were, Ledgor's nerves were being put to the test, for she seemed determined now to cause only trouble.

Ledgor saw her float down and enter a crack between hut beams hardly big enough for a mouse. Silent at the bootlegger's only window, he watched a form that was far less human than the one he'd seen in the graveyard. She was a glowing ball, one that loosed a lone appendage, used for rearranging an array of taxidermy the bootlegger had ornamenting the floor. Her dim milkness lit around the stuffed swamp cats and raccoons, until at last they all rested in an orgy of kisses.

Waking to this, the spooked bumpkin made signs of protection, jerked into his overalls, and stormed into Ledgor's hut with a club and a roaring eviction notice. Having correctly associated Ledgor with the workings of ghosts, he'd traded the club for a shovel, then the shovel for a rust-eaten sword, and finally the sword for curses and mutters before shutting his door and rechecking the deadbolt.

By some miracle, or maybe Niesuri's quasi-divine intervention, Ledgor had avoided tripping on the cypress knots during his retreat. Finding one now and sending his pig flying, he reflected on this recent phenomenon. The witch had said prices were to be paid, and surely copper, silver, even one gold coin minted in Pelliul was payment enough? But letting his blood into the witch's bronze bowl, he'd felt a slight slipping of the senses, one now fating him with real slips, painful trips, and the subsequent accidental lettings.

The rest of the day was spent breaking brush toward the grave-yard. His priestess had been wise in life, and perhaps such wisdom had remained. If he were to be spurred into action, this was the day. The sow was fat and the new moon approached.

Come nightfall, he was in the concealment of a fallen tree, leaning against the dirt-and-root wall it had made. He was talk-ing to Niesuri.

In her full form again, her brightness lit a wraithful pearl.

"When the pig's done 'er job," Ledgor continued, "this... other ghost, or whatever, it'll summon our Gorsuka for us, or show me how?"

"*He* will empower you with what you seek." Niesuri stared down at her reflection in a puddle. There was perfect familiarity to her face, though her eyes troubled Ledgor, as if once-loved gems had been replaced by near-perfect fakes. "*He* requires payment," she said. "But those wishing to call," rubbing her cheek, "call upon lesser beings, such as I, such wishers are rarely concerned with what payments must be made." She broke away from the mirror. "The night is right."

"I love—loved—I mean, I love you, Priestess." Ledgor blath-ered. Niesuri said nothing. Squirming in his embarrassment, he quickly diverted, "So full moons are no good?"

"Full moons are no good," Niesuri said.

What a twist. It was no secret, the only group that had once been more despised and openly hunted than the Gorsukan Order was that patch of villainous scum who tried to evoke ghosts in the graveyards come full moons. "None of 'em have gotten as far as I have?"

"If you mean bringing forth those obliged not to toil," she said, "some have."

"They followed the rules?"

"Partly."

He was no solver of riddles, and though she'd always spoken like someone who'd read a library, her new way of turning his head to mush made him stir in unease. He wrapped a few coils of the leash around his hand and cinched down his hood. "Time to get goin'?"

"Time to get going."

Ledgor and his pig parted fern and vine. Niesuri floated above, lighting their way enough to keep Ledgor's falls down to three. When they broke through the final wall and stepped onto the path bound for the graves, Ledgor stopped. "Priestess Niesuri." His voice; that hand-scalding tone again. "That night we actually summoned us a Gorsuka, was Matina that girl we saw paddlin' away? The night, you know, that…you vanished?"

"Mouse mist," was all she eventually said, then definitely giggled.

)(

Ledgor's neck hair had sparked as he'd descended the stairs. Down here, this was no familiar ghost, one who'd shared laughter with him in life. This was—this *He*—stuffed down in a marshy crypt and requiring blood, little different than Mr. Metek's heathen gods did for rain or amusement.

There had been a footpath, and then a primitive bridge made of sticks and vine. Starting where the last graveyard grasses met the water's edge, this route presented itself under Niesuri's luminescence.

Down in the belly of the mausoleum, sitting on the bottommost step, Ledgor stared across a stagnant black pool. On the other side was a stone table. On the table was an urn of glittering black glass.

They'd been down here for hours. Niesuri's explanation hardly helped his nerves. Even moonless nights held a sort of zenith, and they had to wait.

Then the moment came. At her word, Ledgor, with the sow over his shoulders, waded into the water. Chest-deep, fording what had seeped from places underneath the swamp, he soon found slime-coated steps that took him up to the table.

"Don't suppose you can hold 'er down?" Ledgor said, patting the pig's head as Niesuri lit the last candle. Niesuri shook her head, arranging another straight line. Shadows now danced on the walls.

"Are you ready?" Niesuri said, looking not at Ledgor, or the animal, but at the urn that now centered a pentacle of burning candles.

As if dared, Ledgor brandished Metek's boning knife. He whipped and slashed the air, coming in low above the urn before completing his sloppy imitation of the Pelat by slipping on slime and cartwheeling over the sow. He hit the water with a bright splash.

If ghosts erupt in fits of mirth, he couldn't hear it. Breaking the surface, he gasped for air, then regripped the leash. He sloshed back up to the table, refusing to look at Niesuri. In a spew of squeals, the sow was opened.

Meaning to simply grab the urn and fill it with the sow's spurting blood, Ledgor was dismayed, then he was frozen in a gripping alarm. The urn refused to move.

The pig's severed head made for a suitable bowl. A knee applied to the belly had pumped enough out of its open throat. Ledgor stood again as blood dripped onto flickering candles.

Steadying himself, Ledgor repeated Niesuri's words, filling the urn with the sow's blood. The incantation was similar to the one he'd used to bring back Niesuri. But it was also uncomfortably different. His words were like the poetry of a lark if whispered by a madman. He glared down at the candles. The incantation was over.

"Priestess?" He kerplunked the pig head and found footing enough to risk looking over his shoulder. She was gone. The candles had drowned much of her glow. Without them, perhaps he would have seen her leave, and perhaps why.

)(

Pauthor and Motty were drunk. This was no surprise. What they had in common was precisely that, especially in Amden these days. Having fallen from the heights of Rehton energy potions, Pauthor had first turned to frogs.

Rumored that one somehow caused the other, around the time that commissioner's daughter had been killed, glowers started disappearing. Few glowing frogs meant fistfights, then late-night murders. Almost no frogs meant turning to the banalities of drink. And that's what the town did—lining the pockets of breweries and whiskey houses in Oxghorde, opium dealers from Pelliul, and the sparse but growing distillers and bootleggers slumping about their bog.

At a dingy bar that didn't even have a name, Pauthor Quithot had met Grubilius Motty. Motty practically lived there, when not eking a living out on the wharf. He had a nose like a hook, teeth like an old crocodile, and the old lech was missing both legs below the knee.

To Pauthor, it was hard to say what was more impressive: Motty's knack for finding the few glow frogs that remained, or Motty's ability to run on all fours. As fast as an arthritic dog, Motty could be seen chasing the dock whores to end with his face planted in their rumps. Or acting as courier from one merchant to another. Or directing Pauthor to a dull glow just outside the graveyard they'd spent all night prowling.

"We may got us some treasure there," Motty salivated, perking up on his hands and nubs like an alerted hound. Shouldering their net on its clip, Pauthor leaned off his spear and headed for the water's edge. Seeing the giants that dwelled in these waters made wading into them a constant affirmation of the will. No less an act of will than pushing himself into that crap bar twice a month, to Pauthor at least, who'd grown barnacles against his own solitude.

If there was a medal to give, though, it surely went to Motty. Not only had it been his idea to search for frogs in areas that were inaccessible by canoe or by raft, but it often required swimming through the water that owned a creature who ran off with most of his legs. Motty somehow drove all these points home at once as he doggy paddled alongside Pauthor: "Next you'll be runnin' ferra commissioner seat." His weaselly laugh faded as they transformed into rock-faced hunters.

The water crept up to Pauthor's nipples and then back down to his belt. Through the vegetation, what appeared to be a strip of land had risen slightly from the muck. On the other side, their drink-blurry eyes had seen a holy glow of yellow. It was as if candles had been lit.

"We gonna be rollin' ferra day an' ferra night," Motty said, climbing up Pauthor's back like a monstrous spider and unclipping their net. Stalking up into the dry land, Pauthor's height bore him the shapes first. He drew back. No account from the men who haunted the night, not from the commercial canal to those busy suffering the Pelats—never had there been stories of glowers colonizing puddles in front of mausoleums. A tug on his belt told him Motty was seeing it too.

"Did we just find where all the little guys have been goin'?" Pauthor asked. It was said partly in humor, but Motty had been smitten aghast by the suggestion. Eyes wider than the missing moon, Motty mouthed frantic nothings. Pauthor had only looked down at Motty for a moment. He had heard nothing. But when he raised his head to join Motty's stare, his heart leapt.

Ledgor was no warrior, but he wasn't going to be impaled on a stake. Somehow, one of Commissioner Qell's thugs had tracked him. Collecting bounties, this spear-wielding silhouette already had one prisoner on his knees. As Ledgor charged up out of the stairwell, the only regret greater than the grand summoning having not worked was that he'd tossed that boning knife in a moment of rage.

Ornamented in deep shadow and the devilish ensemble of a pointed hood, what Pauthor had thought was a wraith careening from this witch-lit crypt was Ledgor, who collided into him with slaps and curses. He knocked the spear from Pauthor's hands and set to clawing at Pauthor's face.

The hooded wraith's plea of "Help me!" had startled Motty, but not as much as Motty startled it by punching it in the groin. Gasping for air, Ledgor throbbed and felt the sudden terror of being outnumbered.

A most desperate fight ensued. Rolling this way and that, Ledgor rose and kneed Motty in the face. Motty felt heat erupt from his nose. Ledgor tasted the salt and copper of Motty's blood as it sprayed into his mouth. Ledgor felt the skin of Pauthor—its owner now trying to choke him—clump and goo under his fingernails. Soon, Ledgor seemed dripping in their blood. And then, despite the pain and the fear and chaos, Ledgor heard the growl come up from behind.

Pauthor thought it was a beast like the one that had eaten Hortence and Vernónn, Motty a lost bear. Then both, united in drunken hysteria: a foul ally to this hooded foe before them.

The three men released one another from their web of strangleholds. Not one among them was ignorant to the peculiar noises that came with living in Amden Bog. Most could be explained by the falling of trees or the mating of crocodiles. But what they heard now, down in the mausoleum, it was the gurgle of red-hot earth if able to speak, the raking of dungeon shackles across sheets of forgotten iron.

Motty swung his net around Ledgor's legs, wrapping them together. "Gig 'em! Gig 'em now!" he yelled to Pauthor. "We don't know what else this bastard's brewin'".

Pauthor snatched up his spear from the mud while Ledgor fought to get free.

All three men's eyes opened like water lilies in bloom—Pauthor and Motty, because the wraith's knocked-back hood now revealed the mere grimace and punctured squeak of a terrified teenage boy. Ledgor for the spear that punched through his chest.

Pauthor watched as Motty uncoiled the net from their foe's legs. Ledgor stood at the edge of stairs leading down to a candlelit abyss. Pauthor unskewered him and watched the body topple.

Pauthor couldn't be sure—with his lungs heaving, his hands shaking, and his face clawed up as if mauled by a cat—but at the bottom of the steps, something seemed to give the body an unnatural, final bounce. The boy landed on a slab which held the candles that had so thoroughly confused them. Putting out most, and for a moment facing down, the body then slipped onto its side. What candles were still lit showed the foolish boy curled up and around a dark object that shined and boiled over with what could only be blood.

)(

"They'll just think that damn spook-worshippin' cult finally killed one of their own," Motty said, nursing his nose. "Did you see that woman?"

After a quick debate, they'd agreed not to go down, but that was not why Pauthor remained on all fours. Taking a break from his vomiting, his head dizzied, not wanting to stand: "What woman?"

"That lantern-lit bitch, on the outskirts while—guess you didn't see 'er, too busy gettin' all infantry on us." Motty only smiled with half his face, and though too dark to see, Pauthor knew that ghoulish leer covered him. "If she was a ghost," Motty said, "it'd be the first I seen since the Chapwyn days."

"We need to get outta here," Pauthor said, rising. "What in the good fuck made that noise we heard?"

"I think I know." Motty's voice ran dead cold.

At the mausoleum's entrance, over its top step, hovered a smudge blacker than the night.

II
WHAT MURDERED BLOOD BRINGS

The act of killing had often manifested in his work. In recent years, those who'd died seemed to find a never-ending array of new and elaborate ends. A gallery of suicides—carefully painting the cup that had contained poison, now caught in an eternal roll across the floor, or two daggers thrust skyward, the viewer's eyes channeled toward the tender flesh of an awaiting stomach. One that really should have sold by now was *Upended Carriage*: sunk in the swamp before reaching Amden, its whiskey barrels afloat, with Oxghorde shimmering in the distance.

But like most artists, Pauthor was often fascinated by that which he did not truly know. It therefore sent him bursting through the brush and leaping over graves when he'd killed that peculiar boy. Sure, that moving, man-like blackness was what first sent him running, but once in flight, his full emotions exploded. It was the proximity that had made his gut wrench—feeling the breast bone break, the spearhead driving through.

Whatever that blackness was, it had to have gotten Motty. That poor scoundrel, scrambling on all fours for years just to be caught in some unspeakable end. Pauthor was sent into a fit of tears as he hastily pushed off in his canoe.

※

He loomed over Motty.

"Don't kill me," Motty pleaded, curled up in a cowering ball. "To live, that's all I want."

"To live," *He* said with a voice like snakes uncoiling. "The three of you have granted me this very want. Now," *His* voice shifted, "rise and be recognized."

When he felt safe enough, Motty uprighted himself to his knees. He strained to see into the shadow, which twitched and rolled, but in pre-human shapes he could not yet decipher the mouth that was speaking or the face that would hold it.

"What do you desire, Grubilius?"

Motty had heard the murmurs on the docks. Who hadn't? Ill-intentioned men would on occasion appear in the graveyard, with far more regularity than the ghosts they tried in vain to whistle up. But by twists of fate and luck, he was now recipient to what they all did their furtive and futile whistling for.

Upon the utterance from Motty's lips, the vines cast shadows. Mud puddles began to shine with a brightening light. Glowers erupted about him, leaping between his legs and into his arms. He fell, laughing, covered in their hopping, fiery yellow.

※

Motty desired way more than glowers, but glowers had got him here, and now he wallowed in them. Yes, they led to the hunt in the swamp, and to this strangest but most fortunate encounter. The surges were sending him to bliss. The surges were also a long-jammed answer into a longer-lingering hole of a question.

Motty still held blurry memories of a former answer. He'd once been a Chapwynite in Nilghorde. While grooming to be a priest, his childhood serfdom had left him with an incomplete but unrelenting drive. With no interest in going back to begging, shoeless, knocking the dirt and dust from his hair, a ruthless climb within the ecclesiastical student order was as necessary as the virginity he'd lied about.

He'd cheated on a number of scriptural exams, and lied again to help feed the growing swarm around two rather effeminate classmates. Their conviction of the abhorrent "man-on-man" resulted in their excommunication. It also meant a robed position for Grubilius Motty. Graduation was competitive, after all. One of the shamed and beaten boys had been directly above Motty in their class ranking. Motty would have been denied his vestments, and who had time to wait a whole other year?

Being assigned his own rod and flock had, for a brief time, muffled the voice inside him that would cry out louder than the wind for his own utter, stupendous destruction. But, once having tasted the jug confiscated from problematic peasants, he knew there was no salvation. Defrocked, he slithered to Pelliul, where opium and pouring chalices chewed him up and spit him onto the streets of Oxghorde. Half dead, in a cart whose purpose or coachman's face he could not remember, Motty finally landed in Amden.

Motty wished for his legs back next. If it weren't for the roaring bliss of the frogs, Motty may have felt disappointment. *He* needed more sacrifices first—more blood, more time to awaken fully from this deepest of sleeps from which *He'd* risen.

Motty thought for a bit on how they could best help each other, then bit into a glower and was laid flat.

𐤖

"The legless lechers gone mad," said a fisherman.

"Gone mad with black eyes and a busted nose, but he found 'em, and in plenty," said a jaw-slacked Rigl farmer.

In a fashionable coat gladly bartered by a merchant in blistering frog withdrawal, Motty strutted on his hands and nubs. "Here ya go, Zorbert. And one for you, Gulper." The wharf itself rippled with disbelief. As Motty tossed out glowers, hands clasped around them and shook. Cheers lifted Motty, carrying him into his favored bar with a hero's welcome.

Who needed another wish when one could barter with such a sought-after commodity? By the time the pint that had sent him spinning was swilled and the burliest among the boozers had deemed himself Motty's incorruptible bodyguard, Motty had accrued a pile of coin under furs and a streaming bolt of stolen silk.

Reminders of old days, for some irksome reason, unusually crept in as another song was struck in his honor. "What is possession without power?" *He* had ominously said when Motty'd crawled out from that mausoleum.

"And what's power without lettin' it shine ferra bit?" Motty said into his beer mug, pulling closer his nearest admirer and planting a slobbery kiss on his cheek.

)(

Closing a rowdy night, Ungerfil Qell would often dare a walk on the wharf on his way home, where, once tucked in bed, he'd drum up visions of whatever pair of legs had strutted into the bar, helping to pleasure himself in miserable solitude. A future artist—self-described—in his lowest moments he'd ponder if such a title wasn't equally masturbatory as his post-bar habits.

He bit his nails and told himself the PCA acceptance letter was crawling towards Amden on the back of a dutiful horse.

And it couldn't come soon enough! The bog seemed to be closing in. Ever since his cousin Niesuri's gruesome and mysterious mangling, he'd developed an especially powerful fear of death. That her murder had remained unsolved only quickened his look over his shoulder for the gnashing of teeth or lurking knifemen.

This fear was perhaps why he always scurried away from the dock whores. With their fetid diseases and loathsome company, they were a sure recipe for demise, no matter how hard he'd tried to convince himself that any given *this night* would be the one when one of them rode him into manhood.

Tonight, his voice sang Motty to new heights. He was lauded by his fellow patrons as "slightly better than a stuck tomcat with its balls cut off." Still, by their morose yardstick, that was sufficient enough for a lead role in the Pelliul Theatre Choir. And who could care what a gaggle of pauperous pickpockets thought anyway? The drinks were cheap, his family's tattling cohorts absent, and yet he couldn't shake the knowledge that the bar was below the presence of even the lowest Qell.

Be damned his family's ludicrous wishes: carrying on the arts of suffering a bureaucratic seat and parceling out subpoenas. Of course he'd have to change his name, but all performers do that. No one would wax poetically about a short, balding tenor whose name held a pot-gurgling sound. *Ungerfil Qell, ugh.* A name change would come later, though. First, the PCA. The PCA meant singing. Singing surely would one day mean fame, and fame meant peeling the stubborn leech of sexlessness off of himself once and for all, and in a manner cleaner than the docks.

What Motty had told him was unbelievable, but not as unbelievable as Ungerfil walking into Amden Cemetery at night without a torch or an accompanying army. As the first line of white headstones passed him, Ungerfil reached into his coat pocket and unwrapped a withered glower. Compliments of Motty, a good knife-slice blasted Ungerfil to sit amongst the graves.

You know, Ungerfil thought, *it isn't so unbelievable. Not once you think about it. That Motty, he was crawlin' in glowers. He knows something! Offered 'em for free, then for money, then to me for a few beers. That and a song. The old lech, he heard me, about the gal at the bar. Who didn't see 'em? Heavy tits but not saggy ones. Just right on that gal. Like watermelons.*

Galvanized by revelation, Ungerfil staggered onward. No way would a half-crippled bum be spared but Ungerfil be sent to his death by this...this wish-granting ghost. If Motty was telling the truth, Ungerfil would have to inform his uncle Murgle, after he'd gotten his fill. It would be simply unacceptable—

He plodded a foot into the water.

—simply unacceptable to let all breeds of other men have such easy access to something as earth-moving as wishes. Wishes, even small ones like the ones granted by this *He*, were only worth their shimmer if others, like the scum who populated that bar, weren't able to also walk about in rubies and gold.

)(

Motty had once been acquainted with the rarely read laws governing how the living must interact with the brought-forth dead. But his brain, addled by everything that can be poured out of a jar or hop away, had left his thoughts no sharper than swamp rot. He'd told Ungerfil to summon *Him* whilst light looked down on the old bar, old graves, and the bog. Motty only remembered later that summoning must be done under moonless skies. It was by pure accident then, after braving the steps lit by the angle of the moon, that Ungerfil was able to summon what had first appeared as a plume of smoke. It was perfectly fine, for some reason, perhaps by *His* unique powers, that this time a moon hung above. The plume took the vague shape of a man.

At first, Ungerfil had sworn he'd seen a dead body. The moon, though, coupled with a pool of black made all down here appear as pale, charnel dead. He repeated this theory in his head, giving himself at least some assurance, despite being in the bowel of a mausoleum, that the floating corpse had been an illusion.

"Ouch!" Ungerfil remembered Motty's instructions, which

thus far fell in line with what this horrid *He* was hissing. A kick from a horse, a paddle to the neck, enough pain could knock a glow-surge right out of you. And so could using a knife on oneself. Digging into his arm a little deeper, whimpering, hearing a hissing *yesss*, Ungerfil bled into an urn.

"Your voice is of the morning bird," *He* said. "Yes, but we must hurt, mustn't we?"

Was sarcasm the jargon of the dead? Long ripped from his euphoria, Ungerfil gasped. A blackness, seeming to come from the oblivion of the walls, grew toward him, stretching over the stairs he'd departed from to wade in waters that matched the looming dark. Hidden from the bewitched moonlight, Ungerfil realized he'd been put in an embrace as a father might give having draped his long arm over the shoulder of a boy.

"What do you desire, Ungerfil?"

To his own astonishment, despite the throbbing pain between his fingers, despite the to-the-moon lunacy of being in a moment right out of a fireside horror tale, Ungerfil squeaked out the maxim repeated by all those who are crazed by women while in the dungeons of male adolescence.

)(

Not a damn thing to do with singing, but prerequisites for the PCA had made Ungerfil parse scrolls about Rehleian history. Back when the land was called Orisula, tribes—*primitives*, as the laws in the cities now required them to be called—had used sun and moon to navigate both the wilds and hours passed with near-miraculous accuracy.

The half-moon had moved, enough for Ungerfil to wonder how much time had actually passed in what could only be surmised as a lapse in consciousness. It was night, presumably the same night, and by the look of his trousers, he'd fought every thorn and bramble after leaving the cemetery to arrive here, on the wharf.

The wharf's lanterns were hung high and strung out to burn through the night. In the absence of the day's bustle, the wharf smelled like the reasons it had been built and sounded the way it had been maintained. Wafts of fish and boiled turtle mixed with the greasy aftermath of men having sweated, hands having shook, and goods from the north having burst on the planks to be defended and pilfered.

A heavy symphony of bugs enhanced the feeling he was being watched.

Dock whores appeared out of the shadow, nearly sending him backwards in a reel.

"Evening," Ungerfil said, composing himself, though such composition was made difficult when he noted the severity of their faces. "Boots. Azalea. Gulper too? What you girls doin' out so late?"

The whores said nothing. Boots, who'd remained partly shrouded and whose face had been elevated over the rest, had been standing on a stack of barrels before she jumped off to land nimbly as a cat.

"Without a grinnin' customer, of course, I mean." Ungerfil's voice fell short of its intended levity, and of masking his alarm. He was relieved to find no mugger when he spun around. Turning back, he saw the three had now fully emerged into the lamp light. Walking like they were strung no different than the lanterns, they approached Ungerfil, not even Gulper taking a moment to break into her famous flippancy when he ensnared himself in an abandoned net and toppled over.

At first he heard feet. Then the swish of dresses cut to allure men, now in hurried unison. But he did not hear a word, not a voice except his own as he let out a most unmanly cry. Lost in the tangles of the net, Ungerfil couldn't have felt hands unbuckling his belt, or tugging on his member, or even more insane, his member responding.

Three wild-eyed women ground atop Ungerfil, filling their loins with his cock and his mouth with their juices. Somewhere in the night his bowels released in a final torment, and a trained voice screamed out, then was unable to scream again.

Ж

The knock on his door had startled Pauthor. Even the Pelats knew by now to leave him be. Ignoring it should've worked, but only provoked the knocker into a fit of frantic banging.

"What?!" Pauthor yelled in Motty's face. He wasn't the lynch mob, he wasn't part of some vengeful cult, but Motty was exactly who would lead either of them right here. That Motty was even off the wharf at midday was alarming. Worse yet, he was sober. "We shouldn't be seen together."

"Yeah," Motty said, brushing past Pauthor's leg. "About that."

Pauthor slammed the door and erupted. "Nobody comes here, Motty! How's it goin' to—"

"Candles lit at midday," Motty said. "Someone needin' a funeral?"

Pauthor disappeared in a sway of cobwebs only to reemerge with the frog-gigging spear he'd committed murder with. "And how many have blade heads like this one? S'pose I could toss it, but . . . then I'd need to buy new one, right? Be suspicious as all hell, someone changin' spears at a time like this."

Motty couldn't hide his amusement, and not just at Pauthor's hysteria. Being here was like he was back in a neglected nook of a Chapwyn church. And people called Motty a bum? He'd spruced up dock barrels that were more inviting than Pauthor's. By nailing some boards and the careful placement of a rag, the vibrant health of the swamp's air had been prohibited from entering this wooden dungeon. Straining through solemn candles, he divined what looked to be a bed hadn't been touched since he'd owned feet. But then there were all the chaotic little nests. All the pots and jars and prisser brushes.

"I was sorrier than shit for leavin' ya there, Motty," Pauthor went on. "I was. But when I'd heard you showed up the next day, I was less sorry…'cause, like it or not, you're a drunk bastard, and your kind has a way of sayin' things they shouldn't. And a boy's dead who shouldn't be."

Women haunted the crowded shadows, hung in paintings as queens and whores and midwives. One bore a wild resemblance to a girl whose mother'd been as much a hermit as Pauthor here, and who'd once brokered Motty to try and scare the girl from her habit of creeping about at night. Things went a bit differently.

Such a pleasant memory stirred Motty so thoroughly that it was playing tricks on him. This girl with the strong, slim body and the bat-crazy mom, she poked her head out right then, brown hair and doll-baby face, from behind a painting, then quickly disappeared behind it again.

"Out!" Pauthor shouted.

Yep, shakes and visions were just a few imps Motty had to deal with when taking a break from the hooch. But he'd just have to suffer. There were big fish that needed frying.

"Ain't leavin' just yet. So you heard, I take it?" Motty said.

"Heard what? I was there."

"No, you prissy-ass painter," swinging around to face Pauthor, neglecting the easel he'd knocked over, "not *that* boy. A Qell, he's dead. Happened last night."

Pauthor picked up the easel. He dropped it again when Motty told him why he'd come.

𝕏

"So you're worried that Ungerfil idiot told others what you told 'im. And *who* told 'im. Raped by a snake, Motty, who else you tell?"

Motty took a long breath. "If Ungerfil told anyone else," he said, "it means our boy you putta spear through—"

"Is down there," Motty and Pauthor said.

"Waitin' to be found," Motty said, "and now there's a dead Qell connected to that old mausoleum. And a dead Qell means stakes are gettin' sharpened. He told a soul I told 'im 'bout that mausoleum…"

Pauthor may have worn a smile, but if so, it was a wry one. "And what does that have to do with me?"

"They'll string you up faster than a fiddle. Said so yourself. The spear. The people who prolly saw the recluse of all recluses paddlin' with a fever from the graveyard. You'll be connected to this. Surer than goose shit's slippery. And what about them scratches all over yerr ugly face, hmm?"

"You son of a bitch, Motty."

"We need to clean up what we can. Help me fetch that dead boy."

After thoroughly thrashing his odds and ends, drumming up fleeting fantasies of killing Motty, Pauthor cooled. "If what you're sayin' is true, that means that fuckin' ghost, a real one, may still be down there too."

Motty crossed his arms. "The ghost goes by *He*. What—seen yet another ghost now? Cat finally got yerr damn tongue?"

"It's just—look, Motty, I've seen things in this bog," Pauthor said, "just as strange as a frog-givin' ghost shadow, but—"

"But?"

"But think it through! *He* may have poofed you a few frogs, but whatever that Qell asked for, pretty sure it wasn't to literally get the shit fucked out of him."

Motty reached into a pocket of his coat and pulled out a dried-yellow frog. "Last one, friend."

X

Laid on the floor amongst the candles, it was agreed.

"And, hey," Motty said, drooling, "who knows, maybe get another little wish outta it. *He* didn't treat me wrong."

His hands still tingling, Pauthor shut his eyes. "Maybe I'll wish for 'em to sew your mouth shut."

"Or for a damn butler."

Pauthor laughed for the first time in what felt like ages. They were going back down there.

𝕏

"Our runner," *He* rasped, freezing Pauthor where he stood.

"Ah, he's good," Motty said. "We, uh, didn't mean to wake you," Motty was staring at Ledgor's body, floating face down and shriveled like he'd been sucked dry by a gargantuan leech.

"You trust this one," *He* said to Motty, covering Pauthor in darker shade, "he who runs?"

Feeling somehow prompted, Pauthor emerged slightly from the jacket he'd hunkered in. "Nobody wants to die."

"How very true," *He* said, whipping shadow off of Pauthor like throwing a blanket, allowing Pauthor's torch to once again dance off the urn. "But you two are quite safe from death's unfamiliar clasp."

"Sir," Motty said in high spirits, shuffling to the foremost edge of the bottom step. "You'll protect us?"

"And more."

Pauthor could no longer put trust in his own senses. Motty was in negotiations with a talking shadow, on his knees like the pious to some promise-making god. What was more, the growing excitement within himself. He was still very much alive. He'd just exchanged banter with that talking shadow too. And wishes?

"Protect and more how?" Pauthor, boldened, earning grovels from Motty about the graciousness of their host.

"Nobody wants to die," *He* said, "as you say, yet they deliver me so many deaths. Such lesser beasts awaken that which is before you, but only to a lesser sleep."

Surprised in his own ability to untangle the bizarre, other-worldly speech, Pauthor had followed *His* meaning. "How come all these folks, then, comin' here to summon you up, beheadin' chickens and such—how come they just didn't kill a man and get things goin'?"

"Those obsessed with death are most frightened to harness its power." The fire crowning Pauthor's torch brightened.

Motty scratched the backside of his breeches, then his head. "Sir, I don't underst—"

"You!" *He* roared, sending Motty into the water and Pauthor halfway up the stairs. "And the one who floats—your blood has returned me. I reward those who better my plight. You are now the safest men either of you know."

"A nosebleed for that! One hell of a trade," Motty said, climbing back onto the steps and shaking himself off like a dog. "Say, speakin' of the floater here, and bein' safe an' all, can we take ol' boy an' get rid of 'im?"

With approval, Pauthor and Motty lifted Ledgor out of the water and up the steps. His weight matched his appearance, Pauthor noted. Too light for a fresh-dead corpse, the blood had found its way from this withered husk.

They took their canoe out a sufficient distance and stuffed the corpse into the base of a hollowed cypress.

"The critters'll take care of the rest," Motty said as they returned below. "We good, sir? Protection, and maybe my legs back?"

Pauthor didn't like *His* laugh. Motty didn't either, though shucked such feelings rather quick.

"When you've brought me to full power, such wishes you may be able."

"I think *He's* saying start small, Motty."

Motty huffed, then made a conceding gesture and wished for more glowers.

"Into the urn, Grubilius," *He* said. Pauthor watched as Motty swam across to the table then crawled up to the dark sparkle of the urn. Pauthor's thoughts were on urn itself. An urn: a device where the dead were compacted and housed, reminding the living of life, yes, but also the absolute annihilation awaiting, one there was no coming back from. Apparently such thinking had always been wrong.

Motty took the lid off, then unsheathed his knife and bore a hole in his thumb.

The place exploded with frogs, hopping up the stairs and diving off the mausoleum's little island to light up the waters. Motty followed after them, right up and past Pauthor, gibbering like a lunatic.

With Motty up the stairs and gone, Pauthor felt the chilling aware of his aloneness.

"And you, Pauthor Quithot?"

Pauthor waded over and then bit into the back of his hand. Coaching the first specks of blood, once up, it flowed as if having been freed. "Energy potion," Pauthor said. He'd intended to specify its maker and potency, but before he could do such things, over the urn, a vial was resting in his bleeding hand.

Cold glass and a familiar cork. It matched with such exactness the ones she used to give him that his startled impulse was to throw it.

Then he sucked it down.

There is no difference—the man who lusts to lay with women finally doing so, the frog addict ruining his entire life, the fiendish murderer burying his blade into flesh reduced to screaming gore… and the man reunited.

Pauthor, who had hopped onto the table, broke the empty vial against the nearest wall, wiping the grime from its jagged shards. Then he rammed the sharp glass into his arm. Filling the urn, Pauthor wished to possess forever the knowledge of how to brew the potions himself.

He granted it.

)(

It was true that *He* wanted those two idiots safe, at least for a while. It was also true the masculine pronoun suited his new avatar the best. *He'd* been drifting in the urn for so long he'd lost his own name. But *He* had been male, and a wizard—that much *He* remembered. Come to power in the olden days, before cities spired then toppled, before the land's name had changed and changed again. Human, as they once called him, but strolling the shores of oblivion had long ago filled the soul with unnatural power.

Time had passed since *He'd* granted Pauthor and Grubilius their silly wishes. *His* favorite had been Pauthor's third and final before being jettisoned from the mausoleum. Maddened and sizzled by the potion, ready to slice off his own arm, the whelp had wished to "fight with swords" as dashing as the one he'd sniveled and called "Vernónn."

Yes, a small amount of time, *He* detected, as undefined as all else. Too weak to fly off, *He* put out a ghostly feeler to the docks where he soon learned Grubilius Motty had been arrested. Now in the custody of some pudgy leader, Grubilius was practically in the noose already. Accusations floated about that Grubilius had committed some offense involving the leader's dead daughter, Niesuri.

This was not the first *He* had heard of her name. *He* was grateful that men and women tried ceaselessly to initiate evocation with fowl and rodent blood. Poured by the drop, turning into the agonized gallons, they'd relifted *Him*, his beingness, up out of nothing just enough that *He* was able to feel another being brought back.

She'd been brought back, and it was she whom *He'd* enthralled to lure that Ledgor to him, to most opportunely feed further the gluttonous urn. Where she was now, *He* did not know, nor did *He* care if Grubilius had been the one who sent her to her grave.

He had greater concerns. As always, *He* now knew the inner mind of those whose urn-given blood still flowed in living veins. Of the two, Grubilius's meddling in the arts of evocation was a surprising problem. And even if Grubilius used none which he hardly remembered, the man was still dangerous. Grubilius hadn't talked, but he would, and much was still to be done before *He* could be known. With plans already being set to interrogate him on the rack, Grubilius would have to be freed.

But this wasn't to shower him with more wishes. It was curious what too many voyages in the nether had allowed *Him* to lose and what to retain. Certain precautions had been woven in tales, even back when *He* was decaying along with the rest of the living. And in such decay *He* had retained the lesson: The Vengeful Slaves or the epic of Emphiliax, whose own helpful brother eventually helped him run off the elder cliffs. Once strong, those who helped you become so must be destroyed, or they would bring upon you your doom.

Those silly cultists had been setting the stage with their captured mice and pet rabbits. But even the ones who'd gotten it right, they'd never dared emulate that which they hoped to call upon. It took human blood! Death is no romantic, and the rules of cheating it hold no espousal to the sanctity of humanity. Blood, offered by violence, and in copious amounts. A bled pig had returned to *Him* a voice he'd forgotten the sound of—and a few senses to relish in two startled fools doing what their hearts would have normally lacked the will.

These men, by a most opportune incident, had helped nurture *Him* to fuller form far quicker than *He'd* calculated. Ledgor, Grubilius, and Pauthor had pulled *Him* up to a crucial stage in his devil-driven development. Which meant they also had the power to destroy *Him*.

He would have solved this the moment they'd come back for that Ledgor if *He* didn't still need to ensure that they, or Grubilius at least, would blabber in the correct discontent ears. More sacrifices, more misguided wishes. Once others began acting as messenger, actions could be taken.

"Safest men," *He* laughed. Grubilius and Pauthor needed to be deader than dreams.

There are moments when what is needed and what is wanted gleefully intersect. For *He* could smell the meager want on Grubilius, whose mortality required the most immediate consideration. And this wasn't just because they were threatening that delegged creature with the rack or the stake. While the two stumbling upon his lair had been most opportune, it was the height of misfortune that Grubilius possessed long-sealed memories that, if reawakened, posed a serious threat.

But that meager want, that stench, was nothing compared to what loathed off of that Pauthor. *He* had surprised himself when he noted *He* hated the painter more. The sulking. The insufferable melancholy. That former lover of Man's aesthetics, now just as fooled by Man's waste, unaware of the precious beats of his own heart. Only if he were dead, then his pouting would be of warrant.

His memories of walking the earth were shrouded in black aeoned waves. But within these waves *He* recalled the rules of food and rest, and the consequences of stabbing your knife into another's back. Yet such rules paled in comparison to the governance of the dead. Moons, or the lack of one, were just the start. *He* needed their blood to come to final form. Not all of it, though *He* would gladly slurp and sip all their warm essence until the deep bottom of his urn was as dry as bone. No, just most of it. Needing their blood but them good and dead—it was the trick that came with returning from beyond the veil, depending on the summoners to first bring more bleeders. Ah, the usefulness of paltry wishes.

His current task, however, while stuck underground and at half strength, was not a simple one. And time was of the essence. All it would take was some pestering white magician, if those were still around, to tell Grubilius or Pauthor of their inherent power over *Him*, and then Pauthor would know or Grubilius remember, sending *Him* back to a meddling, hateful spirit. For those who bring back such a banshee revenant, the rules are simple—rules *He* was unwilling to even spell out in the recesses of his ancient mind.

One of them would alert troublemakers. Soon, torches and pitchforks—to suffer *that* again—would overrun the mausoleum. Those by then who followed *Him* and were intrepid enough to stand guard would be mowed down, for the living obsessed with death were never fit nor particularly able. Leading the mob would be one of *His* remaining summoners, and they'd know. What would have been a black-flame reign would shriek and shrink to next to nothingness.

But one was guarded behind bars and the other wasn't entirely stupid. Getting to them seemed impossible, that is until a man, large enough to block out the starlight, descended the steps. In one hand he held a wrung chicken, in the other a dagger.

"Rid yourself that beast," *He* said, "and open thy veins, useful one."

✕

Lodence's arms crackled with newfound power. Muscles that had always won him women and fights twitched around veins that had grown thick as fingers. He knew he was in the cemetery again, and he knew that he'd been down in Motty's mausoleum too. What he couldn't remember was walking back up the steps or wading through the waters that now beaded off his shirt.

Hunting crocs had made him some coin, but never enough.

As he saw it, ruling out Motty's stupid yarn about a friendly ghost who gave you want you wanted was worth a damn chicken. That bum had to have gotten his hands on something juicy, a lost caravan or some dead rich fucker who had no family and an unlocked door. A life spent killing men in Pelliul's fighting pits, however, or doing the same to one nosey Wardsmen before fleeing back to his home swamps to go snout to spear with her deadliest critters had taught Lodence one thing: best to cover the improbables before getting bloody.

Turned out that Motty wasn't lying! Lodence didn't feel fear exactly, he just wished for money. *His* way of granting it sure was a slow-ass way of doing things, though, and the deal made Lodence wonder if Motty'd been infected by *Him* when he came into the bar like some damn king. No big fuss, though. If it worked for a no-leg drunk, it would work for him.

Lodence walked out, nursing a cut no worse than a casual day bringing in croc skins. With one pissant slice and letting some spook shoot into his body for a night or so, he'd be swimming in loot. His daddy had always said it was the fool who let a wagon of jewels speed by just because hopping on it meant a broken bone or two. Broken bones came with every job he'd done anyhow, so wouldn't the man who weren't a fool take a few risks?

Lodence contemplated this as he strangled the last bit of life out of the jailer.

)(

Motty sat up in his cot. His esteemed guardian had been filling both their nights with a rant about his wife and her sisters that seemed to never end nor come to any clear solution. Having walked into the back room to presumably include the rats into his audience, the jailer had fallen silent.

A hulking man walked in front of his cell, carrying a bundle. Motty's heart jumped. "Lodence?" Motty knew it was him.

Lodence was hard to mistake. One of the fiercest men in the bog, those arms from behind looked like the unearthed roots of a large pine. So what he if didn't face Motty? *He* had to have sent Lodence! And who better?

"*He* did, didn't he?" Motty said.

Lodence opened the bundle and placed empty wine jug after empty wine jug on the jailhouse desk. "*He*," turning to face Motty, "yes...*He* did."

"Say, the guard'll be back soon. Bust me out." When Lodence didn't answer, Motty turned his talk to the jugs. "Off to collect a year's good times all at once, Lodi?"

"Not exactly," Lodence said, now steps from the cell, searching amongst a ring of keys.

"What I tell ya, Lodi?! What *He* do for you? Women? Frogs? It's onto golden shores ferr us, friend. Get me back down there, my next wish is yours. Whatever ya want."

A metal roll and one click later, Motty was free. Scampering out of his cell, he rounded the only bend in the miserable place to see the jailer's feet sticking out from behind a wall.

"Sleepin? Sleepin," Motty chortled, "on yerr big, important job. No worries no more 'bout that ol' witch of yours."

Motty hit the floor so hard he thought he'd been struck by a falling tree. His hands were stronger than most men's, but they were no match for an energumen twisting and tightening the garret around his neck.

)(

Days passed. Word spread. Following Ungerfil Qell, and the screams from the three whores as they were impaled and lifted on their stakes, the jailer's death and what horror had became of Motty, the docks whispered grave times had descended upon the bog. Of the rumors that now kept extra candles lit on watchful nights, it was told Motty had been drained of his blood.

Despite such talk and how the no-leg lech was bound to go out miserable and hard, his fellow patrons at the old no-name bar officially named the place in his honor. Still dripping with red and white paint, *Motty's* now hung above the door.

When Lodence ducked his head to enter, they'd thought he'd come to join them for this lowly but fitting homage. Instead, the man who'd always impressed on them the demeanor of a dumb, dangerous ox soon stopped all upward mugs. Furtive glances grew as Lodence spoke with a slack coolness more fitting for the star-gazers and alchemists of Oxghorde.

Into the silence of the bar, Lodence told the secret of *He*. Laughs were killed by his menacing gaze. Soon, a lone question emerged from the back: "If Motty got them glowers from this *He*, and now Motty's deader than hell, what's to stop any us from gettin' dead later too?"

"You all saw yourselves," Lodence said. "Motty was granted an actual wish. Who other than our dearly departed would be offered such a wonder and then ask for frogs? Motty was given this extraordinary gift, yet, sadly, planned on turning on *Him*, to take for granted the gracious powers of *He*. Simply do *His* bidding. Stay out of *His* way."

Lodence emptied a small bag. Rubies and emeralds poured out, sending men to the floorboards to accrue wealth and howl-ing splinters.

Passing on where to find *Him* to the fishery scum and frog addicts and those furtive few who already knew of the urn—now electrified that the ghost was awakened—cleared out the bar like crocodiles had chosen *Motty's* for mating season.

As the last of the beer-soaked wretches found a canoe and an empty sack, Lodence collapsed. Alone, he violently shook, letting out a gasp that would have alerted help in fairer parts of the world. Amid shouts and cycles of vomit, *He* flew from Lodence's mouth.

X

Pauthor had spun himself into uncharted productivity. A table's webs and clutter had been replaced by a frothing rack. Paint jars could take on low heat, and from the hearth they popped and gurgled the odors he'd smelled once in Hortence's old dorm room.

Stacked paintings leaned on each other, making his room smaller and smaller by the day. Pure, uninterrupted solitude and this genius-broth worked such wonders that he even dedicated himself to the idea of cleaning up someday soon and suffering the daylight to go sell a few. The potion's components and paint supplies, in infinite abundance, was perhaps his next wish. Until then, being yet another common slave to money was the only thing calling him to the outside world.

Beyond his walls, the canoe parted patches of Night Waterlily. Lodence, now returned to his normal self, turned to Quito. "Your paddle hits the side one more time, yerr swimmin' home."

Other than light burning from a window, Pauthor's hut sat a solid block of black. But even that orange square was enough to guide these men in the open night. Gax sat in front, paddling in silence. Until he saw.

"Lodi—look."

"Turna round," Lodence choked, "turna round now."

Given a common threat, swamp men with trained paddles can turn a canoe around as if a pin in the hair of a princess.

Between Pauthor's hut and the water's edge, lit torches gleaming in its eyes, lay a giant in the mud. One of those mythical super crocs Lodence had always feared during his night's work but hoped to one day kill. The same tooth-and-tail beast that had caused so much ruckus two years ago at the rain party, now one stopped them from their appointed task.

The night prior, Gax and Quito had been shaken to their superstitious core. Set to kneel under a growing, talking shadow,

He had assembled new foot soldiers. A promise and a sprinkle of gold would always rally the weak or beleaguered man. But now such men laid eyes on a fabled monster they'd been warned about since being rocked in half-broken cribs. As they pushed to gain more distance, they murmured and cussed about what alternate universe they'd wandered into since Motty tossed 'em a free frog.

Soon the docks loomed in the distance.

Gax said it first. "Don't know if the boss has much magic for somethin' like *that.*"

"Don't worry," Lodence said.

Quito stirred. "Glad yerr so calm now, Lodi, but that ain't the only thing I'm worried about. If we got a ghost workin', well if that's the case, there might be, I don't know…gods fiddlin' about in all this. Maybe evil."

"Evil?" Lodence said. "You mean evil like that damn hermit and his pet water dragon? You heard what the boss said. That shit-britches back there would end all our new luck with the flick of a deer tail."

"Well—" Quito tried.

"Bad. Good," Gax said. "What's bad about fillin' yerr pockets?"

Quito sat on this for a moment, then: "What I'm sayin' is, gods and ghosts are s'posed to all be tied together somehow. What if some of 'em don't like all this and wanna stop what we're doin' with *Him?*"

Lodence had seen men from as far as Azad pray to gods before dying under his axe. God talk was as useless as hunting crocs with a handshake. "If they wanna stop *Him,*" he said, ending the chatter, "they better send one hell of a hero."

III
THE SHAMAN'S TALE

My night couldn't get any worse. After spending all afternoon being pelted by a mob, my guard broke through the crowd and locked them from my office. His announcement only completed my confusion; the commissioners, in what had to be an appeal to voters, were demanding my counsel and were at the door.

They, however, were not the immediate thorn in my eye. My office was a wreck. It was a secret to everyone but myself how terrible I was at my job. Even my long-absconded niece was far better. In fact, Hortence had been far better at all our shamanistic practices. She would have gloriously reigned in my position, though, to our family's great lament, she'd told us all that she simply had to go.

My professional mediocrity may stem simply from my lack of genuine interest in the earth-centered arts, something I had been practically forced into at spear point. I am a fan of reading, though. In my proud library, hidden behind such bores as *Horticulture: Plants, People, and Rain* and *Common Components for Curing Diseased Trees* were outlawed tomes of black magic. When my curiosity eventually led me to realize I could call upon far better authorities, it was a haphazard grip on necromancy that

I at long last developed, one I use to regularly summon the real shamans of Amden Bog.

Though less than in my early days, there are still the occasional blunders. A mislabeled bone, a fly picking the worst place to strut and preen. The result: inconvenienced spirits have pestered my recreational studies of, as noted, dark books, or my further investigations into a bottle of Bleeding Anna.

I never liked loitering spirits, but today I had reason to hate them.

My greatest fantasy was throwing off this dreadful weight. I was a hack of a shaman, and in a town one bad harvest away from losing the clothing and reinstituting cannibalism. The most valuable item in this office of skulls and scrolls was a resurrection elixir made by my late grandfather, Oriel. His reputation as the bog's finest practitioner was reconfirmed every time I pulled him cursing from his eternal rest to help me with fish or famine. It always puzzled me that he hadn't used the elixir on himself, but such behavior may have only underlined his wisdom.

I'd planned on writing clear instructions in my will. The resurrecting broth was to be poured into my mouth, but only after my corpse had been shipped off to some sunny beach far away. The only reason this legal note hadn't been completed was it was a daunting task, choosing a dot on the map of the Other Lands that wasn't rife with disease or still being licked by the aftermath of the Municipal One's spear-gilded tongue.

But such plans were altogether foiled after walking into my office this day. I could have split my own head in two. Some spirit I hadn't put back properly was in the midst of tearing everything apart. And in the hands of this amorphous poltergeist was my iron box housing that elixir. Though I was able to wrestle the box from ghostly hands, it fell to the floor. Though locked, though padded, the white lather dripping out told me my precious elixir had been broken.

The damned spirit fled through a window, leaving me to my

anger. But soon came the mob, which found me lost under scrolls, being yelled at by fishermen that not only had my forecasts been wrong, all wrong, but the dredges of the docks who didn't deserve such divine reward had hauled in more in one day than normally seen in a month.

Even without the night's calamities, the job was killing me. I nurtured a colony of ulcers. Heartburn had set in, and right on schedule, accompanying the Rigl farmer's pre-summer nag. After being unable to summon Shaman Shandi, bowel-clearing diarrhea had lasted for weeks— which almost made a surprise visit when that damned spirit reappeared, zipping out from behind a curtain. With the mob locked outside, my guard had turned his back, perhaps prompting the damn thing.

"Tadpole Ghosts"—as one book refers to them— are what you get the night before a returned spirit is in full form. After fullness, they're back to wispy nuisance, then soon back to nothing. But I didn't have time to wait for such retrogrades. After reflexively lunging for the box, in a moment's wit I pulled from my pocket and crushed a ball of *Ghost Repellant*. The red clay was still crumbling from my palm when Gax turned and gave me an inquisitive look.

Between the strange stories of the fishermen and being uncharacteristically set to host Amden's political arm in my own home, I was but a lone, spirit-flung book away from telling Gax to polish his bronze and inform the commissioners they could come back when I'd exorcised my office's most costly haunting to date.

I put on my raccoon makeup and uprighted my chair. "See them in," I said, plopping down.

My dear brother, Emasil, had purportedly defended my abilities in the past, including, cruel are the gods, my organization. He bit his lip, as Rehtons often do, filing in with the throng of liver spots and carbuncles that sagged out of silks and important tunics. All five had come. It gave me some relief to gaze upon the face of a family member, though caught in a low-grade stew of shock and embarrassment. Commissioner Miniri found a corner to occupy, where I knew he would stand like an amiable corpse. It was this silence that had fed rumors I had long ago put him under a spell. As he was continuously reelected, I found no need to refute such gossip.

I winced at the face of Commissioner Ponnick. That troll—a bumpkin who climbed to power by the bruised mishaps we often see on the face of democracies. The scroll he now toyed with was older than the docks, something I'd likely have to convey, lest it be sized up as wiping-paper for the outhouse.

Commissioner Qell joined him in pilfering through my work, finding a rack of vials teetering on a shelf.

"No!" I cried. "Hold it from the base, don't—"

"Sorry, Shaman," Qell gloated, "looks better on the floor, though, with everything else."

Commissioner Qell—now here was a thorn. An aristocracy in the bog was as laughable as a sprawling desert, but those who wore our meager titles of owners and moneylenders loved the little man. Loved the way a savage fawns over his warlord. Come hard times, it was always the nasally whine of Murgle petitioning for my immediate intervention, if not for my formal removal. He'd once ducked my punch, leaving me to mend a broken hand and sort out his litany of threats. Now that my rack had joined the other clutter, its few unbroken vials were left for me to later strain over, finding their hiding spots under the burden of heavy furniture.

"Gentlemen," Qell said, positioning himself, "I am sure I'm not alone in my bemusement. Are we to keep paying a man, despite his impressive makeup, to keep the natural order when his workspace is in such disorder?"

Rising briskly to my feet was only keeping with the etiquettes that came with appointed office, but it rather amusingly sent the little slug back a step, perhaps appearing as an act of aggression in our long-drawn skirmish.

"Father?" a voice said from nowhere, prompting me to immediately break another *Ghost Repellant* and shoo it away. Every politician in the room stared down at the bits of red, then up at my grimace. The voice, that voice, it had come from the spirit. It also struck me as...female, and familiar.

"Trickery!" Qell growled, wide-eyed, as if he'd been surprised by nothing short of a snake in his slippers. "What trickery is this?!"

I could only shake my head and grin, a most unfortunate habit I did without knowing at the worst times. To my fortune, the disaster that was my office seemed to recapture everyone's attention—except Qell, who eyed me viciously.

When I braved a look in the mirror, I saw what most others did: an overweight man of mid-grade height and age, dressed in the various browns of the tunic-scapula-cowl that bog shamans have been obliged to wear since the dawn of creation. But I worried Qell saw, if I was to reluctantly do his intellect a modicum of credit, the clown behind the raccoon paint, whose plump face tapered up to a pointy head that held no original thought. Even the ponytail atop such a mediocre dome was black as in youth due solely to Shaman I-Can't-Remember's anti-aging recipe.

"Strange happenings, big brother," Emasil said, stepping between Qell and I to neutralize, as an apt public servant would. "Quite strange."

"Without question," I sighed, looking at the surrounding disaster.

"Well, brother, how can we stop it?"

"Emy, a haul of fish like the one they're out there raving on about isn't exactly...why do you want it stopped?"

"He doesn't know," Qell said, then lit up like a candle. "Heard of Motty? He's a dock bum—well, was. That scum had something to do with my nephew's death. The whores we sentenced said Ungerfil was cursing his name. We need you to go to the jail and take a look at what's left of him." Qell strained his neck to scoff at my library. "I don't have to read all these to know abnormalities are linked. Don't look at me like that—that's right, *abnormal*. Motty was dripped dry of his worthless blood. Unfortunately, his jailer, who'd just celebrated twenty years of marriage, was killed somewhere in the process."

I needed to get out more. It was the beginning of summer, which meant what little free time I did have I'd spent trying to solve what I'd coined the "Gorsukan Riddle." Our swamps held a terrific beast, one of which was hauled up and killed a couple years ago before I could get to the Party of the Rains to stop it. Many of its bones ended up right here in this office, even the skull, though that had since been stolen. My current theory is the Gorsuka, this most giant of crocodilians, swim up the Moliahenna to breed. Though suited for an amphibious life in shallow seas, they nest under the waters here. Hatched eggs or afterbirth would be taken care of in a matter of hours by our year-round underwater residents. The only real flaw in my theory is that no young have been seen, swimming out home past the woebegone city of Nilghorde.

As Qell prattled on, spiraling death orgies and corpses bereft of blood sounded like something out of a book I'd read, and the notion amused me.

"And you think abnormal fishing and these deaths are related?"

"Good shaman," Commissioner Lynamattix-Qell said, "it's as if a mad djinni from Azadi myth has been unleashed on our bog."

"Nothing I've observed, or the waters have whispered," I was sure to throw in, "has pointed to anything supernatural."

"Ever heard of the Order of He?" Qell said. "Of course you haven't. It's some cult, and it's on our doormat. It's centered on some ghost they apparently just call *Him*. We're confident it's sucked up those reptile worshippers who escaped the stake. Those types, and a whole lost list of our usual mouth-breathing malcontents—pardon me, Commissioner Miniri, I mean our *constituents.*"

"Bored enchantment chasers," I said. "I get solicited by them often."

"Bet you do," Qell said. "More than just chasers, I'm afraid. My dimwitted nephew…his mother is chewin' my ear off. The whores all stuck to the same story; they *couldn't help it* and *were puppets on a string*, that—" ensuring no females old enough to vote were in earshot, "—that one with tits like watermelons kept saying." The commissioners chuckled and wheezed. "And besides all the events of late, stalks of Rigl taller than elms—thankful though we are. Why, a merchant was just crushed by a pile of gold. The murder weapon has been moved to the treasury, pending further study."

"Super-substrate causes larger Rigl," I said. "Muck-gatherers find patches of it from time to time. It's even a plausible origin for our native Giant Crawfish." To mitigate the silence that followed my most unmoving explanation, I began the arduous task of placing books back on shelves and bones over the correct placard. That cherished elixir, my ticket out of so many constraints, had long evaporated. Fighting back the reemerging anger and despair was assisted by the peculiar questions afoot. Odd events did seem on the higher end—like all five commissioners being here.

"And the pile of killer gold?" Commissioner Ponnick sneered. "We need get on top of this. We got a reeeeal talker on a stake this afternoon. We'd debated after, maybe hiring an Ordrid from Pelliul, but my esteemed colleagues talked me out of it. The buzzard would likely sense our vulnerabilities and rally here an outpost of that wretched House."

Though having been an apt wrestler in boyhood, my violence had always been contained to bear hugs amongst brethren or the occasional hurled book. Our bog's dependence on impaling those fallen from our graces struck me as old-worldly and cruel. "A man impaled." I laughed. "His testimony is as useful as," pointing out the rack Qell had broken, "that."

I caught what Qell tossed me. It was a crocodile claw. Then I examined it closer.

"Between gasps," Commissioner Lynamattix-Qell said, "our confessor had said a rather imbecilic fellow he associated with had wished—wished, mind you—for a giant snapping turtle, to keep as a pet, a guardian, or what have you." So much time in Oxghorde had warped the speech of this more tempered Qell. Shucking off his proximity to snakes and brashness seemed to have come from burying himself into law books. He pointed his cane at the mammoth claw. "We dispatched our guards to the premises. The giant turtle was speared to death at last, but we have several funeral arrangements now to attend to."

"Seems maybe some wishes are comin' true," Emasil said.

Before shouldering Ponnick to make his exit, Qell said, "I don't care if you have to impale yourself to conjure up an answer or two. If this black magic isn't coming from *you*, then it's comin' from somewhere."

In my hands was a specimen unlike anything I'd ever seen. Tubercles, even on larger ones, were maybe the size of an acorn. But this rough bump I ran a finger over was the size of a soup bowl. "Black magic wouldn't give us turtles or fish in our pots. It would turn men against themselves, and each other."

"Go see this Motty's corpse, brother," Emasil said. "You'll see the latter."

I needed to ask for a raise.

✕

I was alone once more. Gax had snapped to, escorting them out and shutting my door without having to be asked. I continued the great task of restoring my office, but with only half my heart, which I soon abandoned altogether to pull out a favored book that had somehow remained unaffected.

I sat on my desk and thumbed through the mad escapades of

devilry. Pernicious sects, usurping natural law, blood lettings—all fit the makings of a worthwhile tale, even if a genuine eruption of black magic wasn't behind it. But, given the final testimony of those whores and that claw, could there be such things here?

Our bog was in no shortage of strange tales. The most recent was drummed up after the Gorsukan corpse had been chopped to pieces. As loose, conspiratorial yarns are often weaved, the brutal and admittedly mysterious death of Qell's daughter, Niesuri, had been connected to the "water dragon," or whatever boorish names the people insist on using despite my once-labored seminars. It was the odd timeline that led everyone, Qell included, to come to such knee-jerk fusions.

Back then, I had felt a crumb of sympathy for the man. Tapped to assist, I ruled out our usual beasts when what remained of her was delivered to my office. Niesuri's flesh hadn't been torn apart by great, cheliped claws. Nor would a crocodile leave behind a ghastly pile, as the report had indicated.

I'd nurtured a Gorsukan theory, but of the boglings who go missing each year, which in total could populate a ghost-like, underwater city, pardon my literary proclivities, the issue is obvious: their bodies are never recovered. If there are victims of the great beast's diet, we're unable to point out what final scene the beasts may or may not leave. Thus, we still hunted a human menace, one I'd grown to hope the impaling stakes had sated. And if I knew Qell, I knew dissatisfaction with that hunt was ultimately driving tonight's words.

An old bookmark had gotten lost in the pages; painted endearingly with girlish care. Seeing it brought me to tears.

Had it really been almost thirteen years? Odd, discovering my dear niece's gift as my thoughts were orbiting Niesuri Qell. Even putting the two in the same jar made me shudder. I longed for her, my favorite, my potion accomplice, the closest thing to a child I'd ever had—that young girl whose disappearance had put a black blanket over our family. We'd hoped for the best, with her love for Pelliul and consumptive passion for art, all too familiar, that perhaps she was still alive and well. But such hope had no place in the heart where wishes whispered a foolishness.

Though glancing at the pages, I was pulled away entirely when I saw. Idling in a corner near the window, the spirit was back.

Slipping off my desk to furtively make my way, soon I held a purple ball. Like the repellents, its corpuscular shell housed a tiny galaxy of chants and medicines. Unlike its smaller red cousins, I'd never used this grapefruit.

Oriel, as I'm sure you've already guessed, taught me how to make the concoction. The exercise was done only under a firm promise I'd never use it on him. If I happened to recant on such an accord, I was threatened with being given a case of Thina's Poxy so terrible I'd run headlong into the mouth of the nearest crocodile.

When I broke the ball, a bang like thunder filled my office, with an accompanying flume of purple smoke. Through it, I saw a glossy box appear and then suddenly encase my ethereal nuisance.

The spell must be excruciating. The spirit shrieked, carrying the box to and fro, nullifying my efforts to have uprighted lamp stands. With every bounce against the ethereal glass, the shrieks became more and more a young woman's.

There hadn't been a shamaness pulled from her ashes in ages. This spirit had been one of my blunders, and it had cost me my after-death vacation. My gestures became simple: hands out in front, closing together so the box would correspond. It shrank accordingly. Soon the gloss imprisoning the spirit was the size of the iron box she'd lusted after.

The fight was over. I had her. I took down this spirit-prison from midair and set it on my desk. On my knees, I eyed this spectacular pain in my ass.

"I do hope you enjoy this new home of yours." I said.

"Please," she cried, "release me. I heard everything. My father spoke many truths."

"Only truth is you aren't going any...Niesuri?" It was as if my roof collapsed.

"Yes, at least that which of me is beyond rot."

"How?" I stuttered. "Why?" Stammering until I'd collected my questions into some semblance of order. "You wanted to be resurrected?"

Her voice poured forth as I found a position better suited for not falling over. Who could have forgotten? The prized heir of one's public nemesis, once lurked about in this very office, all in the hopes of spying Gorsukan wisdom I could have only wished to have possessed. I'd fancied her frivolous, sophomoric at best. Besides, having Qell's daughter spend a string of evenings in my company had swollen me with a sort of devilish, one-upping glee. But as was perhaps my life's unyielding theme, I had misjudged her. During one of her many reconnaissances, she now explained, she'd peeked in on me; the half-drunk windbag carrying on with himself about life after death before stuffing the elixir back into safe keeping.

But she had far more to tell. "Nobody is sorrier than I that your potion is gone. I need to go back, with Ledgor, to send back that terrible thing."

"The Order?" I lobbed in pure befuddlement.

"*He* tricked me! I felt him, pulling me." She started shrieking again. "*He* lied! Nothing was to happen to Ledgor, and I was to be recloaked in new flesh."

"Who is Led—why be resurrected, though? Most want nothing more than for me to let them go back."

"It wasn't for me. Ledgor was one of the very few who c—"

But her mad orchestral vision was lost to me. This was all too much. I didn't remember hitting the floor.

X

Waking from a horrid and lucid nightmare, a calm voice was speaking over me like the feathering of rain. "I would have splashed water on you."

On all fours, then struggling upright, I steadied myself.

"This is real," I despaired.

"And we can stop it," Niesuri said. "Concede to their plea. See the body that's waiting for you at their jail."

"This can't be happening."

"Claim it, then bring it to me."

X

Aside from my oath of office, there were perhaps less praiseworthy reasons to investigate the commissioner's *He Order*. Morbid curiosity is as good a motivator as any. Their insistence I see this corpse in our outhouse of a jail had been amplified by Niesuri's.

But when I embarked the following morning, my curiosity was soon spun on its head. A hallucinogenic fairytale ran amuck. As my guards paddled us onward, the Rigl sprouting from a farmer's protrusion of mud were indeed taller than elms. Heads, large enough to cast shadows the size of houses, conglomerated in a new canopy above docks that were swarming with harvesters in lavish garb.

"What time's tea?" a man jabbed, adjusting his golden sash. "Should—shall we bring tha good wine?" A cluster of ruffians roared as two owner-class boglings sped past.

Unbelievable. Fishermen hadn't just hauled in record-breaking nets, nor had the farmers and muckers just discovered super-super-substrate, but the most villainous or disenfranchised of our bog had apparently found great tombs of buried treasure.

"Ever seen such madness, Gax?"

"Looks like Lady Luck's on 'er head with her rear end showin'."

My brutes had a habit of providing me with amusing metaphors. "Ah," I leaned forward, "and some probably want that lady
to cover her shame."

"Don't get 'im started, Shaman," Dorpho said from my rear.

"Not my place to say so, sir," Gax said, "but I reckon, just
talkin' plain, things are best fer some when worst fer most." We'd
reached our dock.

"This way, Shaman Rehton." A uniform sprang to life to jingle
keys and lead me up a path.

The jail, more a wooden house with barred windows, sat on
a parcel shared only by the few ancient trees busy towering in
drier earth.

The jailer—a boy who being granted such a role had to be
part of this mass enchantment—escorted me through an ill-staring
throng of guards and filled my ear about what awaited.

"Nothin' like I ever seen," he repeated, "just please, I been
ordered to tell ya, sir, please avoid the lily-pad-smellin' slut. Don't
even go near 'er."

My laugh surprised him. Though a bachelor by choice, the
choices that comprised my virile years would make even the most
ardent deliberationist dabble in fatalism. My female interactions
lately were reduced to a screaming dead one in a magic box.
The last thing I needed was the ship-sinking chaos of unbridled
women, especially on a ship so old and out of practice. I assured
the lad I'd steer clear as he opened the door and assumed outside
the statuesque pose he must have practiced all morning.

Inside was a wooden room disrupted by sparse office furniture. To my left, the wall was a series of barred cells that ended
prematurely. I could tell there was a room beyond its corner, and
this Motty, unseen, must have been placed there.

"Yerr Shaman Rehton?"

"I am," I said. When I turned to see who was speaking through
the bars, a young woman stared at me from the perch of her cot.

Handsome, with hair that, if not matted and wet from perspiration, would have unfolded off pointy shoulders like an auburn cloud to grace a lean, muscular back. "And you are?"

Her pursed lips gave her a reptilian look. "Matina."

"Why are you in there?" I couldn't help but ask.

"Town's lost its head, now it's wantin' to take mine off right along with it." Though she was rough, and uncouth, and dirty, she gloriously bore the age where womanhood is conquering the former girl. It was ironic; though responsible for the fertility of the bog, I was barren as Azad. As she continued in that twang found deep in our jungles, I oscillated between concerned and shamefully aroused.

Taking a step closer, I saw she was nursing a bump on her head. A chain, clasped to an ankle, ended at an iron ball beside her. Though she had old scars running up and down her arms, most interesting were the dart marks from what could only be the bog's Plumbia frog. Its boiled skin was the crucial ingredient in the family's sleeping broths, as well as a cruder form, used by hunters of both man and animal. It was apparent she'd just woken up from a brain-blighting sleep.

"You been good to my kind," she was saying.

I assumed she meant a fishing family, maybe a confederacy of them. "Oh?"

"Sometimes doin' nuthin's the best a man can do."

"Nothing?" I snorted. "Nothing indeed." I'd fallen for a set of batting eyes. But this critic was caged like a rat, and I could pace around at leisure and barrage her with all I'd compiled for Qell on some cataclysmic day. "If it weren't for me, this town would—" Whatever choice words I may have used were drained from me as I stepped into view of the horrid corner. "Excuse me," I must have said.

There had been a look of severity in the commissioner's eyes. I had even detected a slight tremble in Emasil's voice, counterpoint to the naïve and morbid excitement in that jailer boy's. All at once, it was perfectly clear, the insistence I come here, while now perfectly unclear as to what it could all mean.

This man, Motty, was suspended in the air. Though missing his legs below the knees, the age on those stumps showed them to be traumas received long before this one. A slice across his throat, as was beaten into my ears with every prior report, had deprived him of his blood. "They must've turned him right side up, then pinned him after," I said to myself, for his arms were stretched above his head. His hands were wrapped together at the wrist by what appeared to be some choking device, hanging him in place by way of a convenient hat hook. Left to hang like bad laundry. The sinewy flesh that had once lived tight against Motty's chest and ribs had been filleted, making crude wings that stretched outward, their ends slammed to the wall by daggers. But this wasn't what made me shiver in fear or quell my stomach of its revulsion. By a peculiar onset of rigor mortis, his mouth had frozen while upside down, now a wide *O*, like the most malevolent scarecrow to ever send a child screaming for its mother. Yet it was far from empty. I could only wince and check my own, for his genitalia had been removed then relocated.

I stepped over the half circle of crude charms and bobbles that had been placed below him. Once I'd fought back fits of throwing up, I examined this most mangled of corpses.

This was no work for a shaman. This was for a team of inspectors dispatched by the Metropolitan Ward up in Oxghorde. But I knew, as I stared into the vaginated hole that stared back at me, I was going to be tasked with this nightmare until it either killed me or ran me out of title and pension.

Something I had heard a commissioner say on their way out began to make sense. Not sense in the arithmetical way, but considering what I'd witnessed this morning, reports that this man had been tossing out glowers with impunity was corroborated by his lungs and his liver. The latter riddled with years battered by the bottle, the former being on clear display. The one frog in our parts driven toward extinction even faster than the Plumbia, the Soolorb—or *glower*—left on its user's organs distinct yellow spots. I examined all the little sunflower markings made by a life getting zapped by those lovely creatures. All sorts of magic was kicked up about them, but for all the lore, their lights were no different than mating fireflies, and their most highly sought "blasts" were merely defense mechanisms to escape predation by way of huge doses of transferred dopamine. Most potent of all was its dying jolt, expending its stores and sending men from the earth, up to the clouds, and then eventually down to a grade of Hell.

"Whatcha lookin' at, Shaman?" the prisoner said.

"Nothing," I said, composing myself, "just more dull work for the old fish conjurer."

"Can't be too dull. They," whipping her hair and pointing her chin at the door, "they been comin' in an out all day, gawkin'." Despite her little spat of caustic humor, I didn't like seeing her in here. To the gods, our bog was full of enough thieves and brawlers to fill twenty jails. Why a young lady? It's not my proudest admission, but I knew all the local whores, and of those still left after the Ungerfil affair, she was not one.

When she lifted her ball and chain, I'd stepped back. When she got on her knees against the bars, those eyes batting and shining, I found I'd stepped forward. Was she really asking this? And of me? Was I, a public servant old enough to be her father, really considering it? I saw the ring of keys hanging on a nail. "I'm no pervert," I bellowed, completing a moment of middle-aged idiocy. I was considered courteous, sporting the banal etiquettes when prompted in formal settings, but at the end of the day, I was still but a man. "I can't let you out."

"Just a simple trade," she said, pulling me by my belt to the bars and lifting my tunic. "Some stranger's keys ferr my lips."

"Yes, but…I'm sure you are a good girl—"

"Very good."

"But—unnhh—they'll know. I'll be like a boy with his hand stuck in the cookie jar."

"Then ya better enjoy the cookie."

I fell silent as she worked. Holding onto the bars as to avoid my knees buckling, I fixated on a scar running down her cheek. After some time, I think I said something.

"Like that?" she said, wiping her chin.

"I—I can't," I said, peddling backward and breaking eye contact.

"What?"

"I can't give you those keys." My thoughts shot back to the guards. Thankfully, a commotion had erupted outside. "I'm sorry," I sighed, looking for a hole to crawl in or a rock to slither under.

"Ya better go." Her eyes seemed to glow with a veil of gleaming yellow.

I left, without Motty.

)(

I scurried home to spend an afternoon in angst-ridden conversation with my grandfather.

"What is this *He* business?" I asked.

"In the box, who?" Oriel's shape floated above his summoning pentacle. "Under that blanket, on my desk." He was sure to add. "You fool."

"I'm Niesuri!" the blanket shouted. "Free me from this confine!"

Spirits laugh, trust me—Oriel's did, and at Niesuri's expense. Turns out those disturbed writers I've enjoyed so much had gotten it right: indifference and humor can magnify after the worms have had their way.

Satisfied, Grandad told me a tale that sent me spinning to find parchment and a dip pen.

During his tenure, a spirit had appeared, possibly reappeared.

This *He*. Posing a threat to the bog's fragile balance, Oriel had labored over ways to confront this obscurity. During such labor he went so far as consulting a Chapwyn priest up in Oxghorde. When the sanctimonious zealot learned Oriel dealt in earthy magic, the great shaman was called blasphemer, shunned, and had the door slammed in his face. His own research proved almost equally in vain—almost—leaving him at long last with a location of the spirit, concession of his limits, and a makeshift plan.

Mustering the sum of his powers, he pushed a mausoleum into the jungle—which apparently wasn't far, but when have you known anyone who could move the very muds even an inch? This, and he called up the jungle itself, to enshrine the walls in vines and the concealment of hanging branches. After this astonishing feat, Oriel brandished his renowned present-mindedness and shelved the matter.

My own mind then pulled to the present, for I noticed my office door was closing. Had I left it open? My call for an answer provided me with nothing, nor did poking my neck out into the hall. I heard boots on my porch, right then, at a run, that I was sure. I locked my door and leaned my staff where it would be within reach. Solicitors were common as cabbage, but when I saw Gax next, I made a mental note I'd task him with a good look around.

The moment Oriel dispersed into clouds, Niesuri reconvened her pitch. By the time the smaller clouds had whisked away to vapor, she had practically rattled that useless blanket off her prison.

"Get—me—out—of this," she howled while I sank into my chair. "Let me out, I'll tell you more."

"You know more? More than who you just had the pleasure of listening to? *Ha!* He's the one that made that elixir, you know?" I couldn't help but chuckle at her expense too.

But I soon cooled. She knew more, she said. How prudent was it really to outright deny the counsel of a spirit regarding what was ultimately a spiritual matter? If this "He spirit" had somehow returned, it seemed plausible Niesuri and *Him* might share limitations I could benefit from learning.

My negotiations with imprisoned women, alive and dead, were beginning to make my skin crawl. I leaned forward. "Tell me."

"Two others were with Motty. Find just one."

"And what use are they?"

"Only a blood-giver can send *Him* back. This is why I needed Ledgor." Then she said something that made me want to jam daggers in my ears. "I just don't know yet precisely how a blood-giver actually gets rid of *Him*."

"Oh, that's wonderful. That's a big help. You went after my elixir, *the elixir*, and didn't know what you'd do with it—other than you need one of these legless summoners recently sprung back into action?"

"Ledgor had both legs."

"Enough!" I uprooted myself to pilfer through a cupboard for the right liquor bottle. Returning to my seat, I took a sinus-blistering pull, then another, then made a gesture for her to continue.

"Bring back the body of Motty, find the body of Ledgor, or…find the other man. We need at least one before we can do anything."

I scoffed. "We? If I *do* let you go, about the last thing I—"

Until then, what swam within that ethereal glass was mainly shifting waves of whitish purple. Now her face appeared, familiar and sulking, fit into the pane like a portrait. I found myself stricken with a new grief. "Do you want me to go get Murgle?" I sighed.

"No," she at long last sighed, even more pitiful than my own, sounding as if she'd been encaged for an age of humiliation. "I can't bear he see me, like this."

My relief was palpable. If she could assist me in whatever manner she ployed, her father might be able to harness his executive powers and further our resolution about this *He* business. However, despite Niesuri's death-surviving vanity, there was a far greater reason to not call Murgle here. Regardless of any calming explanation she and I could lay out, his daughter's spirit captive in my devices would surely end in my ruin.

"It would do no good."

"I couldn't agree more. And you?" I said, "Am I to believe you're a force of good?"

"Such things are not removed of their fog once going where I have gone. But," the box lit up, "I was called back, against my will. Before even enjoying the sight of a tomb flower, I was enthralled. Life was taken, and in the fashion that makes angry ghosts, Shaman. If helping send *Him* back to what awaits me renders me a force for good, than yes, I am."

Shame and fear left me with no desire to revisit that jail. Motty wasn't an option.

She explained who Ledgor was, or who he had been, rather, and where I could find him.

⟩(

The following morning, my plans to start the day uncharacteristically early were derailed when Qell stormed onto my porch. There I stood, armed with my staff and a satchel filled with the contents of my best cupboard. Yet I was unable to march off to what would probably be my doom. Instead, I was accused of yet another conspiracy. This one, however, I could only scoff at after the initial wave of sheer panic had left me.

During the night, that peculiar girl had escaped from jail. I almost launched onto the tips of my toes to triumphantly retell how I had not, in fact, honored our arrangement.

My silence as Qell squawked was probably the most prudent thing I had done in a full day and a night. Jailhouse guards were missing, both presumed dead. The others had been asleep when *it* happened.

A jail wall had been obliterated. Slobber and claw marks on the wood gave an appearance that something had shouldered in from the marsh and eaten her.

There wasn't a scrap of flesh left or drop of blood on a plank. Even the largest crocs left strands of their victim's hair twisted around branches.

Qell and I rarely agreed, and I used this moment to nod and concur to the point of ridiculousness. Someone busted her loose. Whoever she was, there were others who wanted her, perhaps so she couldn't talk about whatever caper had landed her in there and since had killed her themselves. My theory regarding skilled carpenters able to mimic claw marks destroyed our brief alliance.

I could not deny the allure that strange creature had on me. Had on me still. If she hadn't enchanted me with her eyes, her curious simplicity, and, well, other attributes…

"Is something funny, Boraor?"

If she hadn't enchanted me already, getting one over on Qell catapulted her to the status of a minor hero. He wanted her head on a stick, even more than my own.

"See!" Qell yelled. "You're smilin' again! In on it, you are. When I finally put this all together."

After much pride-swallowing and assurances made, I was able to corral the man so he could finish his story, for I was curious. I had said my initial silence was probably a smart move, and I say this because the guards who weren't missing had stuck to their concoction: the jail seemed to crack then explode. Roused to their feet and to their spears, from the debris came a giant crocodilian, but not a croc to the letter, with the young girl apparently in the new prison of its stomach as it slithered into the water. This was a consensus they maintained up until their dying breaths but an hour ago.

The only clue left besides all the mangled wood was a drag made in the dirt. It looked like someone "employed a boat with legs to pull a chain and level the wall," Qell said.

According to Qell, hiring new guards was the least of his worries. The no-goods must have been scheming since the moment he'd made the mistake of ordering them to secure the jail. It was perhaps this collusion that angered the commissioners to unanimously vote to burn what was left of it to the ground. If it weren't for this delegation, he would have been at my doorstep sooner, I was reminded.

"Did she do anything to that corpse?" I asked, fixated far more on those guards' unintentional reports of a Gorsuka sighting.

"We'll be burning the place and Motty along with it, but not for a day or two. Is that enough time for you to earn your salary?"

"You know I'll try, Commissioner."

"If you can restore order *and* find that little bitch, Boraor, I'll get down on my knees and blow you."

〤

The mausoleum sat off the edge of the cemetery at a distance that justified Grandad's former powers. Enlisting Niesuri's instructions, I found a path made of leaps and accompanying stick-bridges, and soon I was on the tiny island.

The upsurge in callers had given me reason to believe my home needed more protection than I did. It would only take one more freak event, one more towering Rigl— this time hewn and crashing onto an entire family—then it would be hurled torches, and my wares would be up in flames. But descending the grim steps made me reconsider leaving my guards behind.

The blaze from our afternoon sun lit my passage well enough. A lit torch was just good policy, and from its fire I saw below me a black pool. Where it met the bottom step, shrouded in black, lumped over, was what I took for the corpse, this Ledgor. Shimmers winked at me from his mass.

Braving the remainder of the steps, I saw this corpse to be nothing more than an assortment of wine jugs, most of them broken as if from a fall. They all had loops around their necks, as if to facilitate a group-carry by means of a long stick. I soon discovered such a stick floating in the water, uplifting my investigative senses. I surmised a grizzly fact: the jugs had been filled with something's, or someone's, blood. Wiping the brownish jelly from my fingers, I peered into the gloom. There stood a stone table, barren and old.

It's curious how an angle can change everything. I turned to begin my short climb, as empty-handed as when I'd set out on this fool's errand. It may have been the position of the sun at just the right moment, but now I saw the soggy boot prints that I had tromped over on my way down. They led up, as if someone had first risen from the pool or toiled at that table.

Bending low with my torch, spore from the Anita Nila told that someone had been down here, and recently. Nila grows where it's dark and where it's moist. Such a place was matted. Under several prints I had managed not to tread on, its spore was a lively red, a color only rendered within a single day of it being crushed. This gave me doubts that I'd entered unseen, encouraging me to hold my staff at the ready as I made my way out into the waning daylight.

I'd hoped to return with a corpse, one for a spirit to fiddle with. And with such a convention, maybe some answers.

Niesuri had told of a third man involved in the vile summoning. Presumably still alive, I was to look for a man that was "lanky" and "clothed in garments of the alone." One being just about every man in the bog, the other a description that made me ponder how much the dead actually see.

Yet she'd given a final bit of information that, when combined, had left me with an idea. This third man had trafficked with Motty. That Motty's innards were that of not only a Soolorb addict but a drunk of the most unrepentant sort, I had a place to start.

By the time I'd reached Wilbor, it was evening and my back was sore. I hadn't paddled anywhere myself in seasons. The acid that had accrued in my shoulders sizzled as he yelled I go away.

"Wilbor," I rattled the door, "it's Boraor. I need more than a bottle today, I'm afraid."

A peek beyond the edge of the door showed what one would expect in such a hut: bottles and amateur taxidermy nightmares littering the floor. But overpowering the floorboards lay, no—*pulsed*—the husk of some beast the old bootlegger'd dragged out of the swamp and skinned alive. Such cruelty could have only been prompted by the sudden reemergence of Gorsuka talk. All was fair game and menacing threat in such days, though unfounded. I pushed my way in to tell him this but was stopped.

"Good day, Shaman." Wilbor was seated with his back against the wall. His voice was as grim as his eyes, which followed my downward stare. No skinned beast, jutting out from between his legs, his penis had grown into a ghastly, torturous limb. It went down to the floor, under a table, completely around one of the table legs, and finally ended somewhere under a rattling cabinet. At certain places it was the girth of a man's leg, but in others this demon phallus grew monstrously wide, reminding me of a snake having settled to digest its kill.

"You're writing?" I said in disbelief. He put down his parchment to fight back a lone, bitter sob then, to my amazement, remind me of my mother's adage to be careful what you wish for.

What occurred from that moment to nightfall remains a quilt of memory, sewn together but in no good order. Perhaps this was from my nerves being pulled tight like ropes on a torturer's rack, or perhaps someone, somewhere had "wished" right then for my increased befuddlement.

Wilbor confirmed—yes, *He* was real, and had granted him this disastrous wish. Dark humor was not an attribute I'd hoped to learn an unleashed spirit possessed. Nor did I want to learn what

I already knew: that after many futile attempts of easing Wilbor's fears, I could not reverse this devilish spell.

At long last my composure returned. From the cup of my hands I strained upward to see starlight waiting for me through the window.

Wilbor held a crude sword.

"You made the best stuff in the bog, Willy."

"Better than Oxghorde Gold," he said, "and yeah, I knew Motty. He nobbed around with that painter, the one who lives out'n Pelat country."

When he bid me go, I pushed off, trying hard not to imagine all the blood pouring out from those unnatural veins.

)(

I had a mind to go straight to my brother. Omitting several sources, I could have him gather the commissioners so I could disseminate my findings. *He* was real—had been for ages, right here in our bog. And *He* was back. Three men did the summoning, one possibly still alive. That mausoleum was used for something too. This was surely enough, for I was no detective. The Ward could lend some of those for a few wagons of Rigl.

But, wishes? Pardon the moment of family blasphemy, but even Oriel couldn't do that. Could a wish, if given in perfect unalterable terms, be granted without killer whores or suicide-inducing cocks?

I deliberated on such things as I paddled in darkness. Everyone had at least heard of Pauthor Quithot. If there was one man in the bog who shared my affinity for the beautifully macabre, this great artist was surely he. A renowned recluse, this man of drive and genius appeared in town only on rare occasions to sell his works. It was during such a transaction that I'd once met him. A number of his pieces, regal interpretations of my family and our craft, hang proudly in my home. That he had been palling around with a frogger, one somehow tied to an underworld where excessive drink met summoning evil spirits, this notion only bristled my curiosity. It was like a bony finger pointing me to a gift box wrapped in shadows which grin and frown. And I had to open it.

Strange, then, that a man who lives alone would have two canoes. I pulled up between them and made my way through thick mud under the torchlight before climbing onto his porch. I had always hoped to be able to just talk to him without the wharf's swarm gawking around us. It was no secret I admired his work, but my admiration for him as a man was less spoken of. Pauthor Quithot was, after all, a nonconformist who lived disenthralled from our town's obligations. I could only hope to be so free.

I beat on the door, then pressed my ear. After much rapping with my staff, impatience finally prompted me. The door swung open, revealing broken hinges, as if my kick hadn't been the first of the day.

After enough time had passed for whatever banshee or lunging knifemen that may have screamed through the doorway, I peeled myself from the porch wall and entered a large and ill-lit room.

I was greeted by a labyrinth of paintings, all propped against each other or saddled in easels in varying stages of completion.

The string of reasons to faint was given yet another pearl when I pulled a candle from its holder to inspect what appeared to be the current focus of the madman's work.

I felt I had fallen into a well of dreams, all swirling together in a remaining obscurity. This girl, that fellating escapee, she now sat on a swamp log, centered on the largest canvas, with eyes that owned the world. A short walk revealed a flowing theme: this girl—no, this woman—riding waves of water lilies or in positions so provocative they'd make a dock whore blush. I had to wonder, had Pauthor become familiar with this strange girl in the same bizarre ways in which I had?

Then I turned around.

Its smell still lingering on my clothes, the mausoleum again loomed. Oppressive, *alive*, if I had to describe the painting. A grey, blockish face growled at me from any point in the room. Going up and over a bed, to rid myself of such a line of sight, brought me to an alchemy set that bested my own. Confusion and annoyance waged war in my brain as I recognized all the components and mechanical necessities required for energy elixirs. My kin had told me Pauthor used to inquire about this very concoction. It appeared someone had taught him.

Nearby stood a fireplace still turning embers into ash. Next to this I discovered a rear door, cracked open.

Outside awaited only night air, thick with the choir of frogs. In early summer, our showers take a turn for the sporadic. Such one pitter-pattered on leaves and pooled in the mud. On these surfaces, torchlight lanced off as I heard, out in the distance, someone was talking.

I followed a decrepit boardwalk until it disappeared into the mud. One step forward having swallowed me in the jungle, I hardly had to strain to discern several voices murmuring to one another.

A tree covered in the giant leafs of the Kolucadia served as my roof, and my shield. Peeking around it, a gust of rain tore past me then settled. In a small clearing, close enough for me to extend my staff and touch the big one, a grizzly scene had been unfolding.

Though their arms and faces were hidden in shadows and a nefarious lather of soot, their physiques shown them to be decidedly male. The largest—the size of a damn canoe—stood with his back to me, holding their lone torch in one hand and with the other clutching against him something a reflective black. All three men were staring at a fourth, hung upside down by a rope and flailing like the emerging imago.

The upside-down man mumbled around a gag. His hands were somewhere behind him, presumably bound as he tried to ungulate away from the approaching blade.

"Droppin' and breakin' the jugs cost us, Jax," I thought I heard the big one say, for the rain had rebounded. "We'd be done already. Torches fixin' to be out. Hurry up. Fill the barrel."

Indeed, there was a barrel, placed under the poor sot. Even from my distance, I could see its bunghole open, staring up like an unblinking eye.

The faces of these villainous scum were turned away from me. When I stepped forward, the softness of the mud masked each footfall. I held my staff with both hands and crept to do what my mind could hardly believe. I made my approach and cocked back my great, turned club. In a moment of pure stillness, I saw the upside-down man's eyes, teary and crumpled, suddenly lock on me and turn wide.

Alerted, the giant turned to see his enemy.

With all my weight, I cracked my staff over the fiend's jaw, dropping him like a bag of Apraz.

The other two were on me before the torch hit the mud. I was able to dodge the main efforts of a dagger, still being nipped and slit by minor contacts that sent me howling. I swung and punched wildly, hitting things I knew not what. Then a club put me on my ass.

The large one, as is the brutishness of nature, must have been their leader. They took my moment of incapacitation to try and revive him. I capitalized on the moment as well.

"See here!" I cried. "See here, Gods of Below! May this smoke claim souls worthy of you! May they rot at the foot of your brilliance!" From my satchel, I'd pulled two *Ghost Repellants* and crushed them in my hands.

During the day, the aftermath of crushing repellants is just some red clay and hopefully an egressing spirit. But in the near absence of light, as these men saw before dropping their arms and fleeing, they become poofs of smoke riddled by cracks of red light engulfing the hands of their breaker.

Salvaging the torch from the mud and the rain, I retrieved the dagger that had stung me and freed the man's hands.

With considerable strain, I was able to cut the rope that hung his ankles from a branch above us, sending him crashing to the mud. Through coughs and tears, he rid himself of the gag, belting out his own curses.

"Pauthor?" I said, receiving a nod as he peeled his legs out of their noose. "I can't believe it worked." And I couldn't. That *Gods Below* nonsense had come right out of a book; a particular line I was always fond of, when the honorable brute finds the wrong religion just before the right battle.

"Hand me that torch," Pauthor said. He used it to find the muddy club, then break the fallen man's skull.

Pauthor handed the torch back. His eyes glowed a mad glaze, the type I'd dreamed up when falling through well-written parchment. Then he was gone, up the boardwalk and vanishing in the darkness long before I heard his back door shut.

There was a dead man at my feet. Despite his face being half obliterated, I recognized the square jaw. Lodence had been a crocodile hunter, one who never consulted me personally but whom I saw pushing off for midnight danger with the perhaps lesser men who did. Still tucked in one of his arms was what I now saw to be an urn.

Black as onyx, I pried it from his limp hand and wiped off the mud. There were no markings. Maybe once I sat down with Pauthor, he could explain why the man he'd just killed insisted on bringing this all the way out here. The barrel I understood.

Blood: its role in all this would be revealed to me soon after. For at that moment, I did two things, the second entirely by accident. I took off the urn's lid. As I peered down to examine its contents, a drop of my blood from a dagger wound splashed down into it.

"*Wiiisssh!*" the foul spirit roared, flying from the urn.

I had felt fear before—more so in the past few days than all the other days in my life combined. But no conjurings gone bad nor near misses with snakes or axe-like pincers roused in me the heart-stopping terror as I dropped the urn and fled from what appeared to be a giant bat.

Tripping over the dead croc hunter, roots of trees, and probably my own staff, I scrambled up onto the boardwalk. My hands seemed frozen, my satchel now cluttered and cavernous. After a great struggle, squealing unmanly pleas, I was able to grab the final *Ghost Repellant*.

The darkest patch of night shot back as if launched from a crossbow, but just as quickly *He* was back over me...laughing.

When I made it into Pauthor's hut, I was immediately felled by fallen vials. Pauthor was long gone, and I was alone, left to guess if that laughter outside was real while staring at the open front door.

When I poked my head through the threshold, I saw only two canoes. One was floating away, the other being paddled towards town.

Pauthor's curses continued, carrying over the water between fits of coughs. He was chasing his would-be killers, whom perhaps I had wounded.

This encouraging thought was soon drowned by the newest in my long list of terrors. In the black waters of this most inhabited bog, I swam a nightmarish distance to retrieve my own canoe that someone had pushed out in hopes of slowing me.

The chase now included me, weaponless and dripping.

My confidence grew as I caught up. Soon the lead canoe, seated by two devilish heads, loomed in the backdrop of Amden lanterns. The night had been kinder to the town's goers; songs and revelry emitted from the watering holes and shops still open. That a confrontation of the most violent and hard to explain was about to entangle on the docks wasn't lost on me. To bat back the aches all over my body, I spent a moment drumming up what I'd possibly tell Qell. He'd never have the ass in his trousers to accuse me of anything again. I saw Pauthor slow, and then the torch shine of the elixir he put to his lips.

I'd closed our gap to nearly a canoe length, but now his boat sped forth as if propelled by five men.

From my dismal view, I watched all three men climb onto the docks. Lit by its ornate windows, the proceeding tumble was a silhouette of legs and limbs, kicking and gouging each other in front of the Grey Heron.

The music that played from within our one and only restaurant clung to my brain the way a bad song does on days of too little sleep or too much drink. The banjos and harps plucked as horns and raucous singers serenaded my misery. At last I climbed onto the docks, flopping limp then recovering. One of the two devils ran away.

It would only become apparent to me later that the music of the Grey Heron and the opaqueness of its stained glass had allowed the fight to remain a secret to those within. But that wouldn't last for long. Huffing and puffing, I dove like a befattened spear at the man raining punches down on Pauthor. My aim, if an air-deprived brain was able, was to wrestle the scoundrel off of Pauthor and take him to the authorities—which I suppose I did. For when I made such a dive, I blasted through the glass, taking the man later identified as Quito with me.

"Brother?" Emasil said. The place now silent. Musicians fingered their instruments. Our crowd of wealthy folk, having grown bloated by wishes, stopped shoveling food into their mouths to watch me try and pry myself from the table, and the unconscious man that lay underneath me. But such an attempt proved in vain.

"Tis I, indeed," I said, pain-drunk. My demented smile grew when I saw Commissioner Qell seated in front of me. With him was a Chapwyn priest who, I'd learn, was of a high cloth. Wined and dined, compliments of Amden, it was the hopes of our commissioners to show our town to be more than a place for bumpkins and their hopelessly regrettable impulses.

"Lookin' for other solutions to our local spirit problem, aye, Murgle?" I held a chicken bone like a magistrate's pointer at the priest, then at Qell. For the first time in the grubby little man's life, he remained silent.

"Are you all right, Boraor?" Emasil asked, initiating what would be the first of an endless barrage of questions.

I tried to rise but fell, re-knocking out Quito, who had begun to stir. "Ansul's ass, am I all right? Never felt better!"

I'm sure I would have wallowed in glee, seeing the look on Qell's face, having just spoken the blasphemy that irks Chapwynites the greatest. But such a joy I was deprived. Exhaustion finally claimed me.

X

Days later I woke with a fever. I was wrapped in bandages to such a degree I could not pinpoint which came from careening through a window and which from the dagger. Bedridden in Emasil's home, I was tended to by his servants and by Emasil himself.

When I was finally able to return home, I was greeted with scorn and hurled vegetables. Those that were caught and pilloried for such an assault on me had blathered a loose narrative that I, though they would not specify how, had put their wealth in peril. It was only once lying down in my own bed that I received the first bit of good news.

A scroll with Qell's seal arrived. Being the grand gatekeeper of all things probate, he had signed off on the last will and testament of Wilbor. Turns out I was the sole beneficiary of his remaining stock. "Nice tri" had been penned next to my name, along with a cartoon phallus like all boys draw, but whose humor and sadness was for me alone.

But the booze-maker's final batch wasn't the last package. Wrapped in the white cloth of the tomb, as per my wishes, Motty's body was delivered and placed in my office. Along with this near-future project were two books, plucked straight from the contraband locker before the jail was burned to the ground. *The Embryonic Sorcerer*, for pure reading pleasure, and confiscated from some recent inbound cart: *100 Ways to Use This 1 Incantation* by the notorious Gormorster Toadly.

Their old owner unfortunately had to share a stake alongside Quito, who bawled and bawled, before telling us nothing. The jailers may have been reluctant to relinquish such works to me, but under the declaration of formal study—causing much angst and chagrin for Murgle, I mused—they released them to me and even polished their leather covers.

I picked one up at random and settled in for a good read. It went well with a glass of my new whiskey.

IV
UPON A WITHERED ISLAND

She—Zenciline—sat, eyes aloft,
At her tower window bright;
The sun, now moon and stars, do burn,
For Zenciline—sweet Zenciline—tonight:

Oh, all you kings and clerics,
And brilliant infantry men,
If just one thing would've been diff'rent,
Oh, how wond'frul our lives they'd been.

If the jungles would have just been a desert,
If the mountain could have only been the sea,
If just one grain could've been diff'rent,
Then, fiercely, how you'd belonged to me.

But we can't move mountains with mere mouse mist,
There be no "Hills, please lay flat and still,"
There be but what we've bejeweled the other,
And my white-hot, iron will.

No, the love I seek, a painter of dreams,
A musician on pounding human heart.
May they paint and pluck this poor darling girl,
And from lonesome worlds depart.

For as lilac as in amber,
And as mourners may linger, turn merry,
As healers have saved our ways and days,
This poor darling girl they'd carry.

Oh, how I wait for this rascally rogue,
This endangered, weary turtledove,
Play for me, heart-pounding symphony,
This artist whom I'll love.

—*The Ballad of Zenciline*

It had been a couple years since Matina had assumed her queenly role. She soon learned how short the summers really were, and that most her kind's time was spent toiling as humans. It was a policy nearly as ancient as they were: no Gorsuka ever told any of the others who they were while in retrograde. Most even temporarily changed their names from gut-welled, syllable-heavy beauty to such human drabness as *Pring* or *Dee*. Matina learned this was a surefire way to ensure they'd never cluster together in rough, edge-of-society bands, thus earning the suspicious eye of whomever was in above-water power.

But this policy came with a heavy price. Matina's first

conscious retrograde revealed her old house had been burned to the mud and that she'd been correctly blamed for Niesuri. With nowhere to go and without the wildest idea of how to spend her time, she wandered. From queen back to…this. Lost, she wept, stealing when unable to catch suitable bait for a makeshift pole or eating alive a host of squiggling snakes, something her human belly rebelled against with pure fury. Snakes or raw Apraz, all between fighting off the men who caught her during her late-night thieveries. Those sneerers, with their various incentives.

It wasn't until the following fall, back in true form, that her subjects tactfully reminded her of a beloved mossy pool in what was an otherwise insignificant bend. The feeding! Shelves of rock were down there; pushes from the bowels of the earth that had become monasteries for delicious, fat-daddy crawfish. And far above them was the cabin. In it was Pauthor, the man about whom Mama had warned her so.

Matina's subjects told her what her mother had told them in the days before Matina had grew in cognition and ability. Wretched, corrupt Pauthor had put their former queen under some strange spell. She'd had a fine meal, two full-grown humans, but having your mind controlled was no station for a queen, nor any Gorsuka. It was perhaps this precautionary tale that had led Matina, the consummate rebel, to Pauthor's mud. To see such a wizard.

Most of the time Matina had watched from the tranquil waters. He'd come out to pace on his porch or stare at the night before shuffling back inside. Never once a woman—just him, apparently working in there with his paints. As spring neared its end, Matina reckoned maybe she'd put some of her own skills back to work and trade nine months of misery for a nice place to lay that little human head of hers.

The next retrograde came, and her first point of business was a girly knock on Pauthor's door. It wasn't hard to pull off, chalk one up for royal calculation. The hermit had the needs of every man, needs she took care of while soon being honored as his one and only model.

Matina's eye-batting soon directed Pauthor to venture out for glowers. First, however, he had to chastise her about it with a righteous indignation that would have gotten a Gorsukan male eaten before his post-mating age. But something about her human form carried with it a regrettable softness Queen Matina could never fully shake. Besides, he retrieved glowers nonetheless…and then soon partook.

)X(

It was the early days of summer once more, and just as in the early days of fall, those Gorsuka who'd developed a form of self-mastery were able to change back and forth at will. The only real constraint was the ravenous hunger that came with transformation. She'd eaten that boy guard, but even after a full day of gulping down gar, it wasn't enough. *Maybe Pauthor'll have some fish cookin' again*, she'd thought, finally swimming away from the sector of her territory holding that lumberyard of a jail.

Getting stuffed in there was her own fault, though. Pauthor had told her how the town had gone mad, that was all. It was her foolishness that demanded to go see for herself. Not just go see, but share in the enchantment. She walked as if in a dream amongst the new drunken kings and queens bellowing merrily under gargantuan Rigl. It was just that someone had spotted her. A dart party had been assembled and had put her down.

No bother; she was free now. Of all the berries to tell Pauthor, sittin' high in the basket was how, when she'd popped up for a breath (and a peek) near that heron place there was all sorts of commotion about a brawl that had taken out all that fancy glass.

"*Mmmm*—that fish is sure smellin' good," Matina said, shutting their front door and wrapping herself in a sheet that hung from a nearby nail.

"If you plan on living long enough to leave for Oxghorde," Pauthor said from behind a canvas, "swimmin' at night might be something to take off the pre-departure checklist." He wasn't too happy about her announcement to leave for the summer, but he endeared her by adding, "Your Wildness."

Your Wildness. She always liked that. Certainly understood how her odd ways had earned it, but it still came off as regal, the best of both worlds one may say. But the man wasn't without his fair share of secrets too. To the gods, no. Whenever she'd pry, all she'd get was snarls and waking up to find he'd rearranged the day's workstation to surround him in solitude, like a boy having made a fort.

Had she offended him again? It was almost morning; that he would be awake was hardly a surprise, these being his most inspired hours. But he seemed all too happy to stay hidden behind his canvas. And then the noises coming from behind it: slaps and stuffs of her bag being packed.

A glance around showed her the cabin had been torn apart. "If ya want me gone," she said, "least you coulda saved yerr own door. A busted-up door, what good's that gonna do?" Met with silence, she marched over and pulled down that fuckin' canvas. "Pau—"

He was packing, but his own bag. His face looked like he'd been kicked by a cow.

After the tears, Pauthor told her what had happened that very night, right outside his own back door, and how he'd scrammed away from the dock fight she'd been so eager to tell him all about. Over the body of Lodence, by torchlight Pauthor reconvened his attack, this time with a foot, and while telling Matina all he knew about the mess he was in. Ledgor. *Him. His* minions. He looked for the urn, but it must have been buried in the mud by the persistent rain.

The poor man's right, Matina thought, *he's got no place to go.* She knew the feeling. This dead man out back would make a great meal later, she also thought—dead meat was repulsive, like cold leftovers to a human girl, but Mahtoola, her plumpest of subjects, would delight in it.

"I know a place," Matina said. "We can leave right now. Nobody'll find you there."

Matina was moved by his confessions, how it didn't just jostle something in him but jostled something in her. But she knew she couldn't return such a—what, favor? Her secrets were too big. As queen, it would be grossly irresponsible. Besides, *confess*—hardly, she had not a thing to feel a tad bit guilty over. They loaded the canoe and set off.

"You are the swampest of swamp rats," he brightened as the wall of jungle got thicker.

Ж

"Got ya! And—hot damn—one of the bastards that busted ya loose!" Moebeck crowed, sheathing his blowgun and flipping Matina onto her stomach. He'd given her a weak dart, a lot weaker than the one stuck in that asshole's neck on the other side of this floating clump of reeds. One, awake enough so they'd feel it, and two, playing it safe were in many ways the darter's lifelong maxims. Weak dart or not, she was bound at the wrists and ankles.

Through an extreme grog, Matina made out the stripes and badges of a jailhouse guard. Behind long, wet hair, eyes needled her like tiny rocks. A pit of bad teeth was in mid-foam: "Yerr outfit, whoever you all are, tryin' to take down the boss—quit squirmin'—it ain't happenin'. *He* ain't gonna allow it!"

Moebeck indeed had been at the jail, hightailing it before the guard force could be rounded up by a larger, more weaponed one and impaled for their collective failure. Moebeck, who had been asleep in the crick of a far-off tree, for he was as foul a guard as he was all other forms of human convention, didn't see what had happened in and to the jail, only hearing cracks like thunder. Nor did he see Matina swallow someone whole, nor her swim off at the speed and ease of a strolling summer. This all revealed itself as Matina felt her breeches get pulled down to her knees.

"Yeah," Moebeck cooed, "slur them words. That drool's goin' to good use come the second go." Sidling against her, he seemed determined to lather up the occasion with gibberish. "If ya bust loose again," he said at her ear, "you can strut on in any time, the boss's new place could use one more wet slit. Yeah, that's it—fight! Yerr stone-cold boy back there knows the place, where old Motty first gave us an earful." He worked himself into hysterical ticking that felt to Matina like the farthest thing from laughter. "Too bad that eyeless little eel, Pauthor—*hah!*—he won't be comin' in for a drink no more."

Not the darters nor the shaman knew it, but Plumbia juice had the bizarrest of effects on the Gorsukan. Though Matina could go from chomping Giant Crawfish at noon to eating Apraz and fried trout by nightfall, her transformative abilities were entirely thwarted if so much as a drop was in her veins. But Moebeck's weapon of choice was also subject to its interferences. Abuse of Rehton energy potions rendered the Plumbia in Pauthor no more fierce than a sleep aid administered by a grandmother and her accompanying teakettle.

As Matina yelled and spat, wiggling her hips to avoid Moebeck's intrusion, the deranged little minion of the Order of He was growling how *He* had limited up the wishing until Pauthor was recaptured. "Haulin' ya both in, hell, I'll be swim-min' in gold."

The paddle served as an apt weapon, finally snapping in two by the time Moebeck's brains had rained a candy pink and red all over.

"Look, you're covered in the dumbest brain in the bog," Pauthor said, taking a break from panting to toss the broken paddle and help her up.

"You're covered in shit."

"He got me while I was trying to, kind of—"

"I know," she giggled. "He didn't *get* me. Thanks."

"Looks like we have two," Pauthor said, furiously scrubbing his own filth from his shirt while eyeing the canoes. "Leave him here?"

"Yep, more for my Mahtoola—hm? Nothun'…just a line from a song."

)(

When they arrived, the sun was setting. They had pushed through triple canopy jungle, so thick they had to pull their burdensome canoes over fallen trees and fierce low vegetation before at last emerging into a clearing that struck Pauthor as something akin to a valley. The last leg of it took Pauthor through a crimson tea of bog water. Nosing up to a small island crowned by a thicket of cottonwoods, the few leaves that still clung to the branches were rife with a horde of festery yellow.

"They don't always look this way," Matina said.

Aside from Pelliul, this had to be the farthest from his hut Pauthor had been in all his life—which was likely to end at any moment.

"You have to be kiddin' me, Matina!" Unreal, and they were going to have to stay the night out here. The dead leaves made for a thick, decrepit carpet. In fact, the whole island suffered a sickly look, especially this floor of leaves Matina was likely a mere breath away from suggesting they make a bed of. And they could too, except for where all the slides and paw marks were. Pauthor eyed the slick, glossy black of the freshly exposed mud. Angered by her obliviousness to the one thing as big a threat as *Him*, all he could do was point out the many, many prints. "What if these giants come back?"

The basking ground was the safest place for Pauthor in her

bog, perhaps the entire world. A smirkish grin stretched across Matina's face. "I'll be sure to tell 'em not to."

※

There was no denying the camp had a home-like feel. Cookery and bed linen rested on and hung over his water barrels. A crackling fire warmed Pauthor's back. From its safety, he peered out into the darkness of this most wild pocket. A flicker of orange out in the distance would set him on high alert. A splash would stand him upright with a ready torch and a paddle.

As the pregnant moon waxed, Matina's embrace calmed him, then pulled him down.

He was a creature needing more than the warmth of a fire. More than even the warmth of humanly embrace. He needed what Matina gave in plenty, evident in her being recruited to model for paintings that would have made her mother go to the canvases with a knife and a fiendish howl. She was never sure how she knew such things, but a man who made himself his own land, his own family, a half-dry speck to perch oneself on while in a big lake of absolute indifference, once vetted, was sought after with the desperation of a lost, wandering child.

But *her* heart had remained stolid. In the past nine months, sure, she'd enjoyed his roused exuberance, his odd fascinations with subjects that would spill out like butterflies loosed from a secret jar...plus, kind eyes never hurt. Yet in her heart of hearts, that place she was unable to lie, it was all just a grand barter for a roof and the warmth underneath it.

Maybe it was just that he'd saved her from another rape. But it was likely there was a rat's nest of motivations insider her. Mama, after all, had detested him. And maybe Matina saw something that her first self longed for in ways now barely recognizable. Mama would have hated it. A transformed queen, she laughed to herself, still with such lingering rebellion.

In their blankets, her sexuality grew a second wick, one that lit cleanly and cast radiance on what had been until then only the darkest of landmarks. For the first time, she gave herself to a man, willingly, and with feeling.

)(

"And now we part," Pauthor soured, flopping his eggs out of the frying pan and onto his plate.

"Not forever, Mr. Romance."

When the sun rises in the bog, when greeted by a horizon unfettered by claustrophobic trees, the sky matches the water with such stilling symmetry, an awestruck observer may trace both pink stripes as wagon tracks on a great, purple world. Matina and Pauthor avoided kissing prior to working the gunk from their mouths that comes with a night under the stars.

Matina turned. "You sure there ain't anything else?"

"Sure as summer's here. Told you everything I know. Probably a few things I don't."

"I'll be keepin' an eye on ya, these dark days." His brow crinkled. Her smirk returned.

"You takin' the darter's canoe?"

"Yep," Matina said, surprising him when she didn't load into it a single jug of water. "There's enough to hold ya here for a bit."

"And that's it," he snapped. "*Fuck you* 'til fall?"

"It ain't that, I just—I hafta go."

After slamming his new seat into the mud, a barrel, whose placement and angle had to fall nothing short of perfect, this pageantry of frustration he hadn't displayed since the PCA days gave way to the other matter. "Shaman Rehton is one hell of a guy." It was dismal and humiliating and weak to task a woman with this, but she'd had a point. Pauthor needed to hide. "And yeah," he continued, "he needs to know what that darter said. I don't know much, but the shaman comin' out of nowhere to plant that big fucker means he's well aware of what's going on."

Oh, he's one helluva guy, all right, Matina thought. *What was that sayin', somethin' about when doin' a good thing doesn't hurt much at all?* When that toadstool-owning, back-paddlin' shaman laid eyes on her again—"I'll send 'im yerr best regards," she laughed, then straightened. "I'll be watchin' over ya."

He pushed her off with a goodbye and soon she slipped through a wall of cypress and she was gone. Pauthor had thought he'd heard a tree fall when she assumed her true form and, after swimming down to hug the mud, sunk the canoe with one blasting paw.

He'd be off there and back in town before long. She knew stalking the peripheral, popping up off the docks at dusk, slithering up narrow streams, doing what she could to trail him would not be easy, but her twice proclamation to keep an eye on him would demand her utmost.

Yet such a demand was necessary, for their mutual oaths that once this mess was all over they'd be together had lit them anew.

That man makes me wanna write again, she mused, parting pedicels and lily pad stalks before slipping into a main channel. What she loved most about her obligations in human form was grabbing a quill and putting her thoughts into words. Sometimes they were beautiful. Sometimes they almost seemed to come alive and smile.

She had seen more handsome men. But cantankerous Pauthor, alone on that little island—skinny, yep, coughing, yep yep—but he wanted nothing more from her than what she was willing to give. *Paulie!*

※

Once the moon had clearly risen, Matina, the girl, walked up to Shaman Rehton's door. Given his recent rise in fame, gawkers and onlookers were a likelihood. A locked door would only expose her, but a half-shut window, that soon got her onto the shaman's hallway rug.

She crept past paintings that looked to be of Pauthor's design. A desire to laugh at this surprise—this odd little hello from, what, her man?—quickly turned to a gasp. The door to the shaman's lair was partly ajar. The light beyond glowed out into the hall, stopping at the lifeless body of one of the shaman's guards.

Whoever had twisted this poor fool's neck had done so with a force rarely seen in those who never crawl.

"Gorsuka!" she heard from the other side of the door. She pinned herself to the wall.

This corpse in the hall meant little. What a shaman may have learned about her kind could mean a lot. Her watery court would be held tomorrow. If the wish-granting *He* insanity had bled out to affect them, this year could demand of her unprecedented ingenuity.

Looking into the room proved as unhelpful as trying to listen. The shaman was at the far end, out of what narrow view the crack provided. He sounded like he was at his desk, talking to someone. Whoever else was in there spoke so faintly that she could only pick out the nasally diction of the shaman:

"If this is so, then all of them are, what, shifters?"

"...contact them then."

"What? That? That's nothing more than an over-sung tambourine, passed down from a long line of folks in my lamentable role who signify the births and death of summer."

"Yes, you can go."

"I release you. . . You're using the door?"

From a far room, footsteps had entered the hall. As the sound neared, Matina could all too easily envision a murderer, stalking the rooms in search of others before returning. Unbelievably, pulling at her heart with an even greater tug, Matina could not identify what she now felt—only something else, *someone*, was coming, and from within the shaman's office.

Matina leaped over the murdered guard and hid under a nearby table. Its willowy tablecloth concealed her. Boots passed. She held the tablecloth still as the shaman's door swung open.

V
THREE SIDES TO THE GRAVE

Grubilius had already lost a career in Nilghorde, all temperance in Pelliul—why not his legs in the grey alleys of Oxghorde? Befogged by the type of insanity that comes with excruciating pain, he tried to ponder what next he was to relinquish. Perhaps his skin?

"We'll be coming for those dice-rollers in the morrow, priest," one of his obligees said. The ghoulish duo had relished in their sawing, giving Grubilius gleeful smiles through blips of consciousness and clots of flying gore.

Grubilius had been encouraged to take up gambling. He reckoned a third vice wouldn't be able to clamp down on him as hard as the other two. Besides, his dive into bad-lit dice rooms was not for pleasure. All he needed was a few good rolls, bound to happen—then the frockless wanderer would have enough money to restoke his fever for lust and wine.

The door was the only wood in his hovel not set to ruin by mold or the diligence of termites. When it slammed, Grubilius was once again awake and screaming.

A curtain became tourniquets. A sheet, reinforcements for bandages that had been administered only to prolong his misery.

There was no repaying, not the debt he'd racked up. No sympathy would be given either, even after somewhere in the catastrophic blur he'd mumbled he'd been a priest.

With what was left of his legs, he crawled onto the street and up into an outbound cart, ending in Amden Bog, where, perhaps to his fortune, missing a limb or two was viewed as common.

)(

"I can't believe it," Shaman Rehton said, giddy as a child, patting dry the gleam that had risen on his forehead. "I did it."

After the shaman had asked his commissioner brother to task every paddle, axe, and cane-clutcher to find Pauthor, the disappointing result had eventually led to this.

The painter had fled the scene at the Grey Heron, disappearing behind fern and vine before the last piece of glass unclung from the frame to become a shard on the floor. So now, instead, the shaman had Motty.

Upon the nagging insistence of Niesuri, the shaman finally humored her, enacting this dubious alternative. Now, spitting and squirming, Motty was alive—a miracle to anyone who might hear about the divine intervention without the skin-crawling experience of actually having to see the result.

In the past, out of the same sheer curiosity that gets boys eaten by animals, the shaman had tried it a few times, *it* being what was crudely and over-pragmatically referred to as the *RRM*. Fusing resurrection and memory spells together had worked, scaring him underneath his sheets, surrounded by every candle in the house, lit until morning.

A resurrection brought them back. But such a disturbing feat, as was this synthesis, actually put the practitioner *in* the mind of the resurrected: to feel what they once had felt, to see what they saw, in their own time, with what had been their own eyes. Darker still than experiencing being eaten alive by a split-wide crocodile, like the first, or lacerated and cooked by a merciless disease, as was the foul case of the shaman's second, Boraor experienced what the necromancer Toadly had coined "being in the mouth of the giant at midnight": you only knew you'd been *in* once you were good and *out*. The resurrector and resurrectee remained one, until suddenly not.

This absence of self-awareness chilled Boraor to his marrow. Such preoccupations had served as hands, ones that ripped the flawed and frail fabric of his proficiency in the Recollection Resurrection Meld. Such preoccupations also resulted in abnormalities.

It wasn't Motty's face, nor his right arm. Those had regained life well. Another part the shaman got right was the torso skin. Having laid the flaps back over the ribs, they'd grown back in an instantaneous seal without leaving so much as a scar. It wasn't exactly the puffed and enlarged ribcage underneath, heaving upward with erratic, wet breathes. What would have called up an onlooker's bile was Motty's legs. Retaining their stumps, the thighs had now fused together, giving the taut yellow skin the appearance of slime-coated cheese.

"Filthy wizard!" Motty spit. "What have you done?" Motty wrenched his head up to stare at the cloth laid across his loins. "Put that there so ya won't be too tempted to be suckin' on my cock, aye?"

The shaman remained silent.

Too much sphalerite, too little hen horn, incantations poured over the wrong body part at the wrong time—all causes of a faulty resurrection. Having borne the brunt of such misbalances, Motty's left arm flapped hideous and uncontrolled, no bigger than a chicken's wing. Retaining straps squeaked. "Lemme go!"

That was the last thing the shaman was going to do. Word had trickled back to even Boraor how *He* was demanding Pauthor be caught. An overlap of Pauthor hunters seemed inevitable, so when a fisherman trying to work for both *Him* and Emasil Rehton was indeed rooted out, those willing to listen to the dirt-faced fisher were battered with a litany of curses claiming that *He* had made a turn for the conservative. "Got restrictive with the wishes, the boss has," the prisoner had eventually admitted. "Boss says we gotta haul 'im in before any more gold and diamonds come bubblin'."

Perhaps *He* had a sense of the arbitrary, or perhaps wanted to ensure his powers weren't forgotten by such dimwitted folk, for no restrictions seemed present when a wave of Soolorbs glowed their way onto the wharfs. Reports claimed the frogs wore smiles almost as big as the ones on those thrusting down spears or greedily scooping with buckets.

The latest crop of Soolorbs wasn't why Motty would remain strapped to a table, though. Boraor felt he had pieced it all together. Whoever killed Motty had left his corpse the way they did to incite chatter. Hard to imagine such a sight would boost recruiting, but if Emasil's latest reports were true, chunks of Amden had joined the Order of He almost immediately after Motty's widely-whispered mangling.

Whatever wealth had been wished up before *His* alleged wish-embargo was still raging in the town. One paddle about showed the smiles of merchants and the gleaming polish of ornate, burdened-down canoes that had just been sold off by the score. But smiles seemed to end quickly. The rich had lost their illustrious perch, and soon the poor had lost their landmark in which to target their envy. Silk and a gold bracer had become silk and two gold bracers. Formerly poor men tilled Rigl plots dressed as kings, while formerly perched men pressed Murgle Qell: the source of the wealth must be found, and the poor weren't telling!

Something was brewing, akin to one of those uprisings in fairy tales where the workers dethrone a grim ruler. Or a grim ruler paints his province red.

Half the population butchering the other sounded to the

shaman like a welcome rain shower, but no chuckle could shuck off his grown fear. What if *He* had found Pauthor? Surely the man would be dead, and the foggy hope of the shaman putting an end to *Him* would be that much more nebulous.

Motty would have to do. He was also, according to Niesuri, in Pauthor's special position of original blood-giver, and he sure as hell wasn't running away.

"What I ever do to you?" Motty said to the shaman. Motty remembered Lodence busting him out, but nothing after. Had the commissioners picked Lodence up and now tasked the shaman with...what? A potion, one to get 'im talkin'? About what?

Boraor looked to Niesuri. "I don't think he knows."

"You should've just had that snickering old grandfather of yours do it." Niesuri's shrillness had unfortunately not diminished behind the veil.

She didn't deserve a response, especially for something so obvious. Using Oriel to resurrect Motty was too hard. Those types of chain complications made for worse mishaps than...

"This," the shaman said, with a gesture as if he'd just noticed Motty for the first time.

"*This*," Niesuri hissed from the ethereal box. "This knotted sack. Looks more like he was tortured and twisted than resurrected."

"This is my fault," Boraor said.

"*Ha!*—who else's would it be?"

"No, not..." but Boraor stopped himself, knowing better. The fault he was referring to was about why she'd become so ill-tempered. He'd been too busy at first, too mercilessly overloaded to ask her, but this morning it had slipped out. No need to bring it up for a second time.

She'd been imprisoned in full view of his lumbering presence long enough to follow his train of thought. "Yeah, again," Niesuri said, "let me die *again*."

She'd remembered fully, the answer catapulted from the vaults of a ghostly subconscious. Being asked "*How did you die*" apparently irritated certain spirits as the crushed-up Albaberry does fish in water who happen to enjoy breathing.

"I was eaten," she had groaned, then straightened the shaman's back with the unexpected and still unexplained, "by her."

Calming an irate resurrection and an irate spirit at the same time was no easy task, but confronting *Him* required such. Motty had been murdered for a reason. And unbelievably, aside from his blood, in Motty's memories they'd discovered a clue.

)(

The test runs had worked well enough. It was a feat of trust; the shaman would shut his eyes, settle in his chair, complete the conduit with his hand, and, with his fingers resting on Motty's bucking head, have Niesuri orate rites he was unable to utter, hoping her surliness didn't forewarn a turn for sinister, and at his expense.

From Motty's mind, a puzzle poured out. The exhausting act of piecing it all together had brought them down a long corridor. How the shaman loathed Chapwyn anything, yet there he would end up, time and time again.

His pre-spell guidance to Motty, the latter tirelessly convinced he had not been dead a week, was for Motty to contemplate who and what *He* was, and what power, if any, did Motty have to combat such a fiend.

Expecting a direct-line, hellish memory of meeting *Him*, the shaman was instead whisked away to Nilghorde, to a time before Maecidion Ordrid had been planted. In fact, that very name became increasingly relevant as Boraor and Niesuri's prodding escalated.

At the correct word, Motty went limp. Boraor exhaled, then sounded a lot like the chanting monks he'd suffered in their last run. "Grubilius, Grubilius Motty, take us, take us back. What is there that we can use? You must."

⚹

Sea wind rarely met with the stagnant air of the Dead Kettle District, as it did this day. With it came the warmth of summer, blowing Grubilius's hair back and his tunic awhirl. His eyes, like polished jewels, watched as scrolls loosed from his grip to scatter amongst the human flotsam busy congregating near the base of the Tower of the Waning Moon.

Of all the districts in the great beast that was Nilghorde, the Kettle was home to the largest Chapwyn seminary. Championed as the beating heart of the district, the corpuscular analogy was slightly rearranged on the streets. Hissed by those outside the sect and whispered from time to time by those who dwelled within it, the seminary—a stout keep rattling from the bang of gongs and the droning of an all-male choir—seemed more a gargantuan tumor, sucking what life would have scurried or toiled in the emaciated district surrounding.

The Tower of the Waning Moon was where especially interesting violators of nature or of man were hung out on display. With such remarkable punishment came Nilghorde's masses, bent on agreeing or disagreeing with the verdict with varying levels of enthusiasm. After a failed attempt to discern if the latest victim of the tower's crowning beams was a rotting male or female, Grubilius made his way to the keep. A small but significant plot, his appointed place of duty teemed with great names and doers. Surrounded by high walls and perfectly square windows, he walked under the branches of an ancient tree that had occupied the cemetery's midsection since Ansul himself had probably violated the scriptures.

Such blasphemy was quickly remedied by self-application of the sternest frown. This humor he'd been unable to rid himself entirely, giving cause to visit several bookshelves on penitence. But this mental outburst seemed unusual, as if someone was in his skull with him. As he carried out his task, condemning himself as prescribed, Grubilius had the oddest sensation now that he was someone else, watching a Chapwyn cenobite slog around a graveyard, meticulously being sure not to pray over the same headstone twice.

He shook off this nonsense by the third or fourth row, ending his rounds to stretch his legs under the watchful tree. He wondered what nearby saints its roots were busy sucking dry. Such sacrilege, he noted with some comfort, felt entirely his own nature.

Preceptors had a tendency to set forth an hour's worth of work that could span a sparse stretch of eternity: assigning tutors in the cellar and towers on the same day, a needed paragraph hidden within the vast confines of a dusty tome, hoofing it from the obligations of the kitchen clear past perfectly suitable tables to perform serfdom on a balcony of awaiting bishops. Then why not task out a seminarian plagued with "warding difficulties" to extra study in the Old Church? For this was his next appointment.

Sitting across the Dead Kettle like a charred skeleton that refused to turn to powder, the Old Church was directly connected to the seminary by way of an alley so tight that the Ward had to dismount when a head needed busting. Grubilius departed the seminary's shadow to enter this cobbled path, immersing himself in a market where everyone seemed to share the same set of eyes.

A former icon, the church's western bricks now served as the back wall for vendors of beads, goats, and aging fruit. He navigated through shoulders and basket-laden heads, taking in whiffs of cooked meat and opium pipes, quickly stuffed into their puffer's sleeves upon seeing the approaching religious figure. These sort of reactions had always tickled Grubilius, ever since the first time he'd witnessed a gutter dweller straighten their rags.

"Boiled Quillups, your grace," a woman said.

Grubilius wasn't sure what sacrilege was the worst: accepting the bowl without parting with at least a coin, as the haggard crone had silently hoped, or not being upset a legendary church calamity hadn't permanently ceased free meals from coming in. The penitence books would need another visit.

Having once been the sole Chapwyn post on this side of the city, the first floor of the Old Church's once-glorious seven was all that remained after a mishandling of reviled ashes. Adjacent tales sprouted up soon after, claiming it wasn't ashes at all but a high-risk name muttered off a scroll by a foolish initiate.

No explanatory rumor could capture the weight of having witnessed an entire building detach itself at the second floor to come smashing down in a cataclysmic storm of stone and mortar. Buildings were crushed, denizens entombed, the surrounding streets lost in a smoking pile of rubble. From the dust, revenants and howling phantoms emerged to walk or fly among the living. Possession and molestations of the most insidious carried on until a dispatch of Ansul's True surmounted the rubble to form ranks.

The Vault of Names still served as the Old Church's basement, overseen by the grimmest priest to ever don a vestment.

"What do the scriptures say of tardiness, Motty?" The priest sat on a low stool, leaning against his cane and leering at Grubilius with his good eye.

"Apologies," Grubilius sighed from the base of the daunting staircase. Aside from the urns and jars and iron boxes with multiple locks, the only objects visible in this tomb were the haunting placement of the candles themselves, all reflecting off Deacon Ulyent's engorged cataract.

"Apologies?" The deacon grinned. "The scriptures? Hardly." Sarcasm had apparently been omitted from the long list of Chapwyn prohibitions. The deacon seemed to imitate a frog trying to hold in a stubborn fly. As Grubilius waded through the candlelight to a wall of awaiting parchment, it occurred to him that this was the foul man's form of laughter.

The Chapwynites hated magic. It struck Grubilius as curious, then, that they wielded a quiver of rites and practices as wizardly as any of those they feverishly plotted against. "I need to go over spells," Grubilius said, then quickly remembered the proper nomenclature—"rites, I mean, ones for encounters with black magic."

"Black magic," the deacon gruffed. "All magic is black." After letting the young student display a devotion to meekness, he tossed a heavy book at Grubilius.

Failing this examination would mean failing the term. *I fuck this up*, Grubilius thought, ignoring the fire growing in his gut, *it'll take treachery black as any damn spell to see a damned robe.* Grubilius pulled up a stool and settled under the glow.

As time droned on, the deacon would stir, never taking his eye off his charge. "The farmer late to sow," he would say, "be the soul early to transgress, lest he toil by long, hard torchlight." As intended, the verse rang in his student's ears the way a mosquito reminds a woodsman that there is a hole in the tent. But by a grace evident of Tersiona, the wretch finally uprooted himself to use the latrine, or maybe just fall in and drown.

"Toil yourself right into a ditch," Grubilius grumbled, taking a break from the Goetic book to pace about and contemplate how miserably he was to fail the morrow's gauntlet. It was unfair. Making matters worse, there was no one to take the blame. Back at the seminary, he couldn't ward off the puniest specter summoned by the most charitable deacon, yet he was blessed with the useless ability to memorize entire pages of verse-covered scroll.

Scrolls. Most down here, he noted, were bound in the seminary's official seal. But one had caught his eye, near the deacon's stool. One that wasn't bound.

Unbound. Furtive. "The road to salvation be laid plain

without mystery," he quoted, bending down, "then the road to damnation surely lie in lusting for the mysterious."

Ansul's ass! If he'd wished to switch sides, this scroll would surely earn him at least his own polished basalt throne in a not-so-bad steppe of Hell. Turns out the church was amassing another morality hit list. Such lists were common in the dining halls and the dorms, but most of that chatter was futile disputes among brethren. The denominations that dizzied the religion had also included what order of trials and public executions would demand liturgical priority.

On most lists, as on this one, Maecidion Ordrid was at the very top. *Good luck going after that necromancer—*

—the student's eyes caught at the bottom of the scroll: "Allegedly dead."

A curious trio comprised this second list, all sharing a hen-scratch note; "*blood-summoned spirits." There was Syphamat Garl and Blagg the Infector, both old nemeses of the church who had, by most accounts, risen from the dead just to be packed back down by a zealot army out near the Red Isthmus.

Grubilius had experienced before the sensory alterations associated with studying the forces of darkness. Reading "Syphamat" made the room smell like sulfur. "Blagg," Grubilius felt his stomach turn.

And there was a third.

When he read the name, barely a mumble, a taste entered his mouth like the copper taste of blood. Next to this name a single line screamed up at him, "Should be dead,, again. Marshes hugging southern step of Oxghorde. Amden town."

The deacon's sandals slid and scratched beyond the candles. Grubilius fixed his eyes on a final note, thick and black in the margins. "Confront this class of spirit w/ their original name. Next break their receptacle. NOTE: original blood summoner/ donor must hold said receptacle before breaking."

Grubilius looked up to see Deacon Ulyent staring at him. As bizarre as what he'd felt amongst the seminary graves, the deacon's face seemed to look like someone else. Deacon Ulyent opened his mouth. "What in—"

)(

"—the goddamn hell!" Shaman Rehton yelled, rising to his feet. "That's it? *That's* the key to all this? Break some sacred object tied to ghosty, flying fuck all! It's right out of a child's tale."

"Metaphysical truth is always found in the tales we use to scare children," Niesuri said, sounding as if, were she alive, she'd be aloofly perched on her preferred cushion, painting her nails.

"Copper?" Motty grumbled, licking his lips.

"I've done all I can, greatest of shamans," Niesuri said. "You'll release me?"

Shaman Rehton was busy reliving a vision of the urn. The one he'd held for but an instant out behind Pauthor's. That was it, had to be, the receptacle. Motty could end this. The shaman wrapped himself around the hope it was still where he'd dropped it, then waved his hands. Niesuri's ethereal prison expanded to the size of a standing coffin.

Almost a perfect image of the girl who once lived. Seeing her, looking in those eyes, Motty saw more than just translucence. He saw the fateful night at the mausoleum, the night in jail, and...

Motty looked at the shaman. "Why'd you do this, Shaman? Why'd you do this to me?"

"We had to, Motty."

"Ghost here helped you?"

"Yes she did."

Niesuri pitied the wretch, an emotion she'd once been largely bereft.

He gazed at her with something like wonder. If she too had been brought back, then wasn't she an indication for some form of afterlife, or continuance, one he couldn't recognize but had to already be a part of? Sure, he'd read most the scriptures, but he hadn't actually believed any of it. "Where was I?" he said. "Where was I when I was…"

"Gone?" said the shaman.

Motty looked at his chicken-wing arm, then returned the shaman's stare. "A man, a ghost…an' me. Guess there's three sides to the grave, huh, Shaman?" Then he was out cold.

）Ӿ（

It was late. If Boraor took his canoe now, he could be back from Pauthor's before sunrise. The place had to be swarming with scouts from both sides. Maybe he could rouse Emasil, show him Motty—yes, he was still breathing. Good. Maybe Emasil could lend him some armored men and storm over to Pauthor's.

"Let-me-tha-fuck-outta-here!" Niesuri pulled Boraor from his pacing. Energized by her confinement's recent expansion, she clawed when not pounding with milky fists.

"I thought you wanted to watch *Him* go down in flames?" the shaman said.

"Piss on that. I sang the songs you couldn't sing." Pointing at Motty: "If you are as cruel to this creature as you were—*were, hah!*—are to me, you'll keep him around on a leash to help with that hideous spirit. I want out. I want out! I want ouuttt!"

"Who ate you?"

"…You'll let me go?"

）Ӿ（

Boraor soon needed his chair once more. "Wait," interrupting Niesuri's rant on lesbian sex that had cartwheeled the shaman, "she turned into one? A Gorsuka?" One thing the shaman could count on was a summoned spirit's disinterest in lying. *But*, he thought, *couldn't they still just simply be mistaken?*

"Nothing gets by you, your druidic eminence. Chased them, worshipped them—hell, wanted to *be* one of them for most of my cut-short years. All to find out." Her words trailed off in a slush of maddened sobs.

"Who was she?" he whispered.

"Doesn't matter."

"If this is so," the shaman said, not knowing if he was mouthing more a statement or a question, "then all of them are, what, shifters?"

Her voice momentarily surmounted its melancholy. "To eat us alive in more ways than one."

Boraor adjusted, mumbling at last, "I need a way to contact them then."

"You have one."

"What?" He followed her eyes to the balial hanging from the wall. "That? That's nothing more than an over-sung tambourine, passed down from a long line of folks in my lamentable role who signify the births and death of summer."

Her laugh resembled a feminine slant on Oriel's after a particularly grand blunder. "And when did I say the Gorsuka are themselves? They are connected to summer as are heat and rain. Can I please go? At last I remembered my own lover put me in my grave. Now all I want is to return."

Boraor read about this. Toadly's seminal work on summoning had stated reliving their demise was the final phase. After that, only shrieking mania. "Yes, you can go."

"You *release* me?"

"I release you." The shaman waved his hand, ending Niesuri's prison with a crisp, sudden *pop*. Instead of turning to vapor, she performed what was perhaps a final act of humanness. "You're using the door?"

She stopped at the threshold to face the awaiting hall and

hover like a bee. "Strange," Boraor heard her say, "but I feel someone is near. Someone I once knew."

Then she was gone.

Niesuri had vanished into thin air. Boraor would have pondered more her sudden change of exit if he hadn't been so utterly consumed by what she'd asked him to believe.

If only his niece were here. "Even part animal," he muttered to no one, giving the fantasy a chance while looking down on a snoring Motty, "still right enough for a *Beast Summoner*. First body that *He* fucker assumes, I'd have the closest Gorsuka swallow him down and end this. Ansul's ass, how I wish I had one right now, I'd…oh shit."

It was just like the ones Hortence used to help him make. A hollow ball of hardened clay, a *Beast Summoner* had appeared in the palm of his hand.

The shaman rarely squared effects to their causes so quickly, but this one came so absolute the onset almost floored him. The blood—his blood, that drop. He'd become part of this. His utterance had become a wish fulfilled.

The door swung open. As if wished for as well, Gax stormed through. Motty came to life, bucking and screaming, "Copper! Soot on the tongue!"

"Speaketh the priest," Gax said, his voice deep and unfamiliar.

"Gax!" The shaman gasped before reassembling himself. "What are you doing here? Where's Dorpho?"

"I went back for my urn," Gax leered. "The one that Ledgor I wouldn't let move."

"What the devil, Gax?"

"When I am in it, it's quite hard to move, you know."

"It's *Him*!" Motty screamed.

New strength accompanying this speech was made known, for Gax bounced across the room like a cricket, burying his dagger deep in Motty's chest.

"Gax!" But a hand on his guard's shoulder only got Boraor tossed over his chair. Boraor heard strange words coming from beyond his upended seat, but when he dared rise, it was the sight of Matina which demanded his complete and utter bafflement.

She, this bizarrest of girls, she stood at the door, also with a drawn dagger. She was here to join Gax in some unholy wreckage of the shaman's work and life.

It was only when he saw Motty hacking up a diminished scream that Boraor leapt up to confront Gax with his fists and his feet. When Matina joined the fray, she did so unbelievably on behalf of the shaman, slashing and poking against bronze armor that sang and screeched with every meeting of Dorpho's dagger. Though Gax would kick or turn one of his larger plates to Matina, he never ceased chanting a string of black words.

At an instant, Motty shriveled to a husk, putting a smile on Gax that began his new task. Matina was no match: her wild slashes countered with playful, mocking dodges, her charges met with hard smacks or a stiff boot. As Boraor watched Gax over-power the valiant girl, he held a thought, however fleeting, that he'd seen and suffered similar movements behind Pauthor's. Gax caught an arm, throwing Matina across the room, burying her under a shower of falling shelves.

When Gax climbed on top of Boraor, it was after he'd pulled him to the ground as if the shaman were no wrestler, but an old and pleading woman. And such pleas were met with deafness, for the shaman saw in those eyes what he'd only seen in nightmares.

Thunder cracked. Flakes and slivers rained down. If his eyes hadn't been slammed shut, he'd have surely been blinded by…bone?

Gax slumped over, writhing on his side.

In Matina's hands was the femur of the Gorsuka that had been killed during the Party of the Rains. She gazed upon her weapon, damaged by her blow to Gax's skull, and then chucked it like it tried to bite her.

In the throes of death, the guard had his shaman beside him. Despite the mess, despite having pummeled, despite having tried to kill, despite knowing he was a fool for doing so, Boraor's compulsion to serve as spiritual mentor lowered him to his knee. There were passages for those who dwelt in earthy magic, and he thought he had begun one. When he had to finally look away from Gax's hideous expression, he found that he hadn't, but rather he'd been uttering, over and over, a protective rite that he'd retained from one of Motty's memories.

Matina and Boraor leapt back when Gax's mouth shot open. "Smoke?"

But Matina'd guessed wrong. The blackness flying out grew arms, then legs, before becoming a shadow, bristling for but a moment with a livid face.

※

"Damn!" Boraor hurled another book.

Matina, that girl's appearance had been as mystifying as that tearful rant of hers still ringing in his ears: *If I'd been myself—but couldn't, not in front of the likes a you, you back-peddlin', swindlin', no-key-grabbin' sorry excuse ferra shaman—if I'd been myself, this asshole woulda needed a whole lot more than slapdash armor.* Afterwards she'd regained her sanity to tell the shaman a thug named Moebeck gloated *His* lair had been relocated. Any other night, Boraor would have likely administered a syringe's worth of plodynal into her most available vein. She had saved his life, however, and arrived at a time convenient enough to reconsider his lifelong goal of never lighting a candle on a Tersionan altar.

There were many questions—this Moebeck's whereabouts, the alleged location of *His* new headquarters, her arrival, her rant and her revulsion over half his collection of bones. None would be answered. As she'd begun to speak with a semblance of coherence, he'd absent-mindedly tampered with his balial. Matina was out the door as if compelled by something right out of one of Niesuri's most riveting but misguided recollections.

"Damn you." The final book in Toadly's collective works had held the passage he was looking for. As he feared, a consultation of dog-eared pages rendered resurrecting Motty a second time impossible. Through the temporary conveyance of Gax, *He* had executed rites far greater than Boraor could ever hope to muster.

)(

Amden Bog got wind of Boraor's latest brush. Rumors of the night abounded, including Gorsukan sightings a toad's toss from the shaman's easternmost skirtboard. More reverberating than the rest were the consistencies, recited with ever-increasing fervor: how a shadow shaped like a man, or a man made of shadow, how it had wailed from the shaman's home to bang amongst canopy branches.

VI
MOTTY'S BALEFUL THRALL

I was tempted by the thought of resurrecting Gax—not just to pry into his traitorous mind, but as Qell's dinner party went on, the idea of the dagger-work I'd seen at Pauthor's home, and then later my own, would have made a satisfying end to all this prattle.

"Oh, come now, Shaman," Qell said. "You could use some exposure to new ideas. Isn't that what you bookish types are always quacking about?"

Qell had a tendency to rest his hands on his paunch when he laughed, reminding me of a seated frog—thus reminding me of the deacon down in that foul Nilghorde cellar. This chain of associative thought perhaps bubbled up by way of Priest Vodaphul. Like the first night I'd seen him, when I'd crashed through the Grey Heron's window to cover him in his dinner, he currently sat next to Qell.

"Most of the new ideas I'd like to explore have been outlawed," I said. "Mostly by finger-pointers, like our guest of honor here." I tried to avoid Emasil's eyes. I knew he was embarrassed by my words ever since this miserable night had begun. But I also knew he was obliged to honor this dispatch of Oxghordians. A bit of damage control was in order. "But those I am still able to parse are quacked over when summoned by the curious," I added, failing, "and the capable."

"Capable of believin' rubbing toadstools together or fish bones on warts can cure or cause the weather," Qell said, perfecting the seated frog. After all the chuckles at my expense had finally exhausted themselves: "Look, Boraor, after that last run-in, like it or not, you're the talk of the bog. My constituents apparently champion you, apparently lavish you—just look at that robe you're getting snake sauce all over! However, as you may already know, Commissioner Miniri's constituents are divided. Of the poorest, there are those who fear harming you would bring about bad luck. Others want you dead."

I was reflecting on his cynicism when I heard Emasil say, "This is for your safety." Of course, referring to the Chapwyn detachment.

"We will do great things together," Priest Vodaphul stated.

We? This conspiracy, formulated behind my back and attempting to finalize without my approval? These dinners got worse with every new moon, but learning the commissioners had hired a wasp's nest of Chapwyn types to "assist with the *He* problem" made Qell's wife's already atrocious cooking border on the unpalatable. It was a doomed wisher's confiscated gold that was used to employ the Chapwyns, and such irony seemed to be this pageant's burgeoning theme. Priest Vodaphul, head of the detachment, smiled at me the way a cat may a cornered rodent.

If Amden wanted the help of Ansul's Thugs, everything wet and south of Oxghorde was already doomed. And if such a lending hand was needed, well, they'd still see such a calamity only after my fat corpse had stopped twitching high on a stake. It was my dislike for their religion that forced my brother to find evermore sooth and diplomacy. Their smugness, their dangerous ideas and condemnations, slamming the door in Oriel's face during a moment of humble request, to now slither down here to, what?

"Great things together," I said. "We?" I fixed my gaze on Qell for I could stand the polished and side-burned face of the priest no longer. "Commissioner, Chapwyn assistance in our problems is unnecessary and, may I add," a couple of brushes with death had a way of liberating a man from the chains of timid etiquette, "unbecoming of our bog leadership, conscripting outsiders to do our housekeeping." My dear brother's face was in his soup, but I couldn't stop. "What could a gawker at books written by virgins know about the Order of He?"

"Blood *donations*" was all Priest Vodaphul said. It was all he had to.

The twitch the priest's words caused me was without explanation. I capitalized on that it forced my head down, avoiding what was surely an unprecedented smirk on Qell. Staring at the lace and embossments fronting my new robe, I didn't merely see *His* urn as one does with their memory, but as my eyes would if also in a...a place made of wood? I was seeing where the urn currently sat, somehow.

"Yes," I said, trying to pay no attention to the way the priest had crossed his arms. "Blood donations. What else?"

"Overfed raccoon!" the priest erupted, causing every spoon to drop and mouths to pucker mid-slurp. "I have dedicated my life to fighting the forces of darkness. What must you hear, venerable soothsayer—the five somatic gestures used to fend off possession, along with their lexical order? A word or two on spirits, or as the provincial refer to them, 'ghosts'? Fine differences between conjuring and summoning more vast in the unseen spaces than the flight between stars?"

It was now Qell who crossed his arms. The priest curbed his froth.

"I want to cleanse this supernatural filth, as you do, not just from your bog, but from the world. Yes, in the name of the church, but for the good of all, too."

This censer swinger, carted down to rattle off in my ear, all our ears, what one trip down those Old Church stairs may teach a pimple-ridden student.

"Surely a man working in cousined metaphysics understands this," he said.

Qell swelled from the confrontation, and soon from the banquet he and the others began remembering was before us.

"Sorry," I said at last, dropping more spoons. "I'm not working with you."

Ж

Ansul's True as your newly appointed protection, please note, feels far more like hymn-humming prison guards. I'd have resurrected Gax forever if only to rid me of this burden.

"Do not shut thoust door, please, Heathen Priest," a guard stated.

"It is my door—virgin—my house, and my heathen office," said I.

By the sound of it, the big one took over. "Strictest orders," he said. "You are not to be let out of our sight," before slipping in a surly, "sir." I eased from the office side. Doing so, the door gave way, giving me great pleasure when at least one of them fell flat on their face. "Priest Vodaphul wants you alive, Snake Charmer," the lout said, clamoring back into his uprighted armor, "which is more than can be spoken of thoust water-logged congregation."

"Piss on your priest and his wants!" Reasserting my efforts with renewed force, I caught them in a lull and locked my door. "*My* office—brutes!"

"Thou art under our iron wing, still," the third one sang.

My tongue would be pulled with holy pliers if I didn't cork this anger, but its release had delighted me. I opted for cracking a few *Repellants* at the bottom of the door, fanning the results under until I heard my captors murmuring anxiously. I chanted a loud, whimsical stream of nothing. As I'd hoped, they took my gibberish for a brewing spell. They ceased all efforts at breaking down my door. Instead, they began nailing charms to it, much to the sorrow of my ears.

※

It was hard to avoid the creeping thought: I was enslaved to this Chapwyn intrusion. Not just by the men outside with their hardwood staffs and clean swords, not just by the teary-eyed plea from my brother or the other commissioners' reminders on duty. I went long swaths of time disregarding the tales of eccentrics, the moth-eaten leather of strange tomes. I'd once yearned to outgrow this fascination, but other than irksome looks at the mirror, there was no indication that time changed anything, and maybe it best I just abandon such hopes.

Tersiona, if she exists, spared me the absence a particular imp. The Weeping Goddess of all that is Good, with Ansul, her first and most beloved prophet, steadfast but whereabouts unknown. The duo had purportedly passed down all sorts of proverbs overseeing pathways out from temptation. If I were to dither, if I were to cast down my people's ways and embrace a foreign, spreading dogma, then I would have to admit that for whatever good I may have done in my life, such paths eluded me. The touch of near-forgotten women, a bottle's call, slips of the tongue, and, chief among them, as I began summoning Oriel, the dark world's lustful pull.

It helped to paddle my mind toward a slightly different shore. Niesuri, or rather her spirit, had provided me with more personal experience than most mortals suffering from my tastes could ever hope for. A pervert would thaw in envy, knowing the titillation I felt watching the post-summoning stages transpire as if right out of Toadly's masterwork. I had controlled! I had used with great success the tools of greater men, and had tasted the ether of spirits as much and maybe even more than my mentors.

So why did the prospect of working with this priest conflict me so deeply? He was the face of something I loathed. Yet Niesuri had proven still not enough, as had all I'd encountered with Motty, from the now-burned jail to his finale amidst the restraints before me. I had to see how close I could get to the dark flame, and Vodaphul, ironically, seemed the fastest route.

⚹

Priest Vodaphul was being put up in, of course, Qell's guesthouse. Just as possible, with how those two had been acting, Qell's bed, kicking Mrs. Qell to the dog rug.

Per request, I headed there, but on my own, out of the custody and clamor of my armed entourage. They were militant, but like all zealots, were as blind to human nature as they were to their own convictions, which made them easy to fool. At least for a while.

When they caught up, they did so panting and lancing me with bitter glares. I was tackled and pinned, until I launched the pinner with a kick from my free leg.

"Shaman Rehton, will you please spare your protectors?" Priest Vodaphul larked, descending the guesthouse stairs. "What would *Pauthor* think?"

"I shall spare them *this*," I said, my anger rising at his sniveling tone. Freed and on my feet, I delivered a kick to the big one's groin, dispelling a myth they were all castrated.

"*No—ahkk*," he croaked as I wrenched down an old favored chokehold that'd put several boys to sleep.

"You called, Priest Vodaphul?" a voice said, a wobbly voice.

Pauthor? Pauthor had spoken as if roused from bed by a bell. My curiosity was alerted before he'd even attempted a step down the stairs. The miserable hounds leveraged on my preoccupation, freeing the lug from my clutches with a sword's hard pommel and sending me sprawling into a puddle. The skirmish over, the priest looked on his men with towering disapproval.

As Ansul's True hoisted me up, murmuring their curses in my ear, my eyes were on the only living blood-giver. The sterile white tunic draped loosely over Pauthor was of the Chapwyn kind. His image was one of abject misery. The bags under his eyes and bruises about his arms and neck suggested he'd spent several sleepless nights being beaten by every vine and branch in the jungle. This notion at first satisfied me, even soothed me. But his demeanor, that bee-in-the-bottle slackness, it caused me grave concern as to who or what he'd encountered since fleeing the docks.

"Here he is, Shaman—stay up there, Pauthor. Here he is," Priest Vodaphul said, "the remedy to our little ailment. Savior of the bog." Then the priest did know how to combat *Him*—at least as much as I did, maybe. I almost blurted out my question whether he already had the urn as I was prodded up the stairs. Bracing myself to find Qell on the other side of the door, I was now fixed on another question: how was I needed if the priest had Pauthor?

Inside, I was greeted by more guards and, more pleasantly, Oxghordian meats and cheeses, and no Qell. Totaling seven now, the priest's protectors—and mine, I suppose—ate as a group would that had been plucked from farms to swing swords and thump the unchaste. Vodaphul sipped and nibbled, joining me to stare at Pauthor. As I observed Pauthor drink little and eat even less, it occurred to me I was now a character in a droll scene much like the ones he painted.

He was far worse off than I'd originally thought. Pauthor's eyes seemed to have been misplaced then refitted once questionable muds and unknown time had been wiped off. His practically undead demeanor made more sense when the priest gloated how they'd captured the poor fool when he'd snuck back to his hut and subjected him to numerous "spell-weakening rituals." The man's brain was whipped eggs.

When the priest snapped his fingers, the nearest goon handed Pauthor his sword. "It is the oddest thing," the priest said as we both watched Pauthor wheel and whip the long blade with surprising dexterity, "but when we originally took the poor fellow into custody, we heard from the waters fronting his hut the most disturbing noise."

This pageant of Pauthor's swordsmanship made sense only if I was to believe I was being shown the priest's hold on the man. I believed exactly that as this blowhard continued: "Growls. Deep gurgles from a disturbed reed bed, seeming to be caused by something very, very large."

"Did you see what it was?" I asked as Pauthor finished his dashing display and was seated without sword or expression.

"No. Oddly, when my men emerged onto the porch with Pauthor, it was as if his hugging and thanking me for the first of the aforementioned rituals placated the underwater stir."

If the priest wanted a shaman's explanation, he wasn't getting one. Nothing to be stunned about here. Whatever charm spells had calmed the man had also obliterated whole swaths of Pauthor's mind, rendering him thankful as a drunk to his charitable tavern keeper.

"And you think this," I said, pointing at Pauthor with one hand and flicking the hardening mud off my lap with the other, "inclines me to assist in your works, sir?"

"Shaman, as you know, our dear Mr. Quithot is to go right into the wolf's mouth."

I think I hid the full bloom of my snarl. He had a point. Even though I was going to lose whatever argument I'd hoped to rally against the holy man, it gave me some assurance at least that I'd given his goon a good thrashing in front of him.

"Priest Vodaphul," Pauthor whimpered, eyeing the plate that had been thrust on his lap, "I don't want to see *Him* again, or his followers." Then he was the man I'd witnessed in the night rain. "You'll have me killed as fast as they would."

"There you have it!" I said, galvanized by finally having an ally. I slapped Pauthor's shoulder. "You have no friends here, Priest."

When not vying for Tersiona's humble throne, his eyes could be menacing. Peeling them off of me, the priest shifted them back to Pauthor. Both said nothing, but I felt as one may having stumbled into an ongoing argument between a father and his recalcitrant son.

"As fast as they would," Pauthor repeated, deflating back to this new, post-Chapwyn self. He slid my hand off his shoulder and hung his head. "You should go, Shaman Rehton."

I was on my feet before the cheese tray I'd dropped had ceased to rattle. Going was exactly what would wipe that shine from the priest's manifestation of arrogance others called a face. After all, I was the one who'd been summoned.

"Leaving? What, no friends here?" the priest said to my back.

I seized the nearest chair. I do believe the priest would have flinched if his guards hadn't shouldered between us with their half-drawn swords. Yet it was Pauthor who stopped us.

"Payments for wishes are horrible now," he said.

"How do you know this?" I said, for I knew it too, just not as well.

"A fisherman," Pauthor continued as if I'd said nothing, "wished his brother walk into a brood of crocodiles. The wisher wanted his brother's wife. But the payment was the wisher's own wife, gutted, her entrails warming the buried urn." Pauthor looked at the priest. "We are grateful for your presence here." Then Pauthor skulked off, perhaps to mumble their scriptures.

I might have asked to borrow one of the nearby swords too— this time to bop Pauthor on his head, as had so efficiently been done to me. Absconding with the feebled man seemed the only moral option, but the priest had put some clamp on him that sat me back in my chair.

"What's really been done to him?" I said.

"He's been partially decursed. Don't worry—sluggish, bereft of character, all common."

"Partially?"

"My guards have caught Pauthor multiple times at night clawing at his window," the priest cocked his head the way a conspiring robber may right before divulging the master plan to their accomplice, "trying to get to *Him*. *He* is calling Pauthor. *He* has grown, you know, in strength and ability."

"I know little," I said, mid-stride, ungluing myself from this stuffy room once and for all. "I can't help you, Priest. I'm not as useful as they sing. Perhaps find that wild stick of a woman, Matina. She seems to possess an entire bag of tricks."

"Oh, you have your tricks too," stopping me where I stood to coat me in a greasy smile, "Shaman Bait-for-the-Pillory. We under the good graces of the church can smell the useful stench of necromancy."

Stench? Such pejoratives should have been the least of my worries. What else did he know? Worse, I knew. I knew that *He* had seen way into a vile, full-tide. I knew this, for Pauthor knew this. Our inseparable link came from the spilling of our blood into *His* urn. Contemplating our horror, I absent-mindedly patted the ball-shaped waste of a wish I'd made, now occupying a pocket in the blasphemous satchel slung about me.

The priest changed his tone. "Will you help? Pauthor would dislike anyone else."

I still wasn't ready to ask what in all the great expanse that was Mulgara it was they wanted me to do, let alone ready to see Pauthor stumble right into *His* wretched claws. "I can't. Pauthor and I are connected in ways you couldn't possibly—"

"Understand? Overfed raccoon you are not," he said. He smiled softly. "Lest fed on compassion. You nor I want Pauthor hurt."

The following morning, I stayed in my bedroom. My companions, a stiff bottle and Toadly's *100 Ways to Use This 1 Incantation*, lulled me deeper into the funk I'd fallen. The charms my guards had nailed to my office door had beset me with an illness no rot-grub nor plodynal could break. It was because, through blood, I had connected myself to the Order, not because I was a shaman. At least this is what I told myself. To their everlasting joy, my attempt to remove the Chapwyn pins and pendants had only blistered my hand and encouraged my submission back into bed.

Application of any theory is strange. Never what one envisions before the pop of doing, the flash of what's arcane crawling through time's tunnel and coming to life before you. No different in Motty's case. I had executed, but I had blundered. According to the pages in my lap, Motty had been an abysmal wreck.

Yes, I had seen it. I needed no page to tell me that what had squirmed and squiggled back to ungrateful animation was the horrid aftermath of a haste-riddled amateur. It was just Toadly's academic approach to the observed possibilities, the incredible spectrum, that rendered me yearning for another go. I sipped on whiskey and perused. A day in bed is good for us all, especially for those of us who enjoy the whiff of unappreciated pages. Unappreciated and pornographic. It was no secret, Toadly's lecherous tastes. That he had them illustrated in the margins carved in iron his notoriety, and, before long, surmounting my age and slight inebriation, made of iron my—

"Become decent, Snake Charmer," a guard said at my door, nurturing my theory they were sent to do nothing more than torment me with divine punctuality. "Priest Vodaphul enters."

"Wait!"

I only had time for one. Opting to conceal my sinful shame over my sinful book, Vodaphul, after scanning my most cherished decorations with artless indifference, floated to my bedside and soon traced the book's title embossed on the cover. My embarrassment, my worry, my anger for feeling both all diluted when he ended the tracing with his eyes to begin following "Gormorster" with his fingers.

"Did you know Toadly is heralded by many as a genius?" he said.

I did. The priest's face wore a calmness that disarmed me. I would have loved to have seen my own, for the shock I felt had certainly made me appear a brainless fool. I stepped into my slippers.

Had I seen him with different eyes? The priest was slightly dirty—vestments smudged, hands beset by labor from days gone. As he surprised me with thorough, enthusiastic retellings of his favorite passages, I found myself weighing, unbelievably, if I was looking at an ally in the skirmish of what is and isn't taboo.

Dignifying myself as best a man is able while caught in his undergarments, I said, "Genius, and a pioneer in his field."

"Several fields, if I'm correct."

"You are."

I partly understand why I snatched the book from his hands. He had, until but a moment earlier, been the personification of censorship, to say nothing of consigning literary rebels to pillories and nooses. His fingers curled, but his eyes remained pleasant.

Yesterday I'd consulted Oriel about the Chapwynites. The litany of long-dead curses alone, I'd for a moment believed, was going to set the charms hanging outside ablaze. Then Oriel's anger cooled, as did his accompanying swirl of dust.

Oriel's parting words had stayed with me: "The worst of evils comes in the cleanest of robes." I knew now why bitterness had shown its crack; Vodaphul was exemplary of an institution laying pressure on one of its own, in ways muffling the spirit perhaps worse than simple, brutish fear. Here was an actor, forced to play the same dismal role each and every day.

Yet if I was to believe he was an adroit actor, what's to say this sudden fondness for the forbidden wasn't the real charade? I held my book.

"You were—" one of the guards barked, marching in from the hall. "We advised he clothe himself, Priest Vodaphul."

"Next time you interrupt a coalescing of brethren," the priest bellowed, "I'll have your hands dipped in oil and you assigned to mission work in north Suela. Never mind their exuberance, Shaman Rehton, their swords are sharper than their wits. Get out!"

When I was sure the last part wasn't for me, I sputtered, "It's okay," then, "I've had worse guards."

Shutting my door for me, Priest Vodaphul said, "About our matter at hand."

He read my eyes.

"Shaman, Pauthor can't do this without you. *I* can't do this without you."

At long last, the secret of warlord victories revealed to me: nothing is more persuasive than potent drink coupled with the charisma of organized religion. I heard myself say it: "I'm in."

His eyes flashed. His lips pressed. He pointed to my settee. We sat, but not before he outdid himself by shaking the syrup from the bottom of a cup I'd misplaced and poured us a drink from the bottle I'd failed to hide.

"Our Pauthor's current state is placid, numb, like a dullard's dream," Vodaphul said.

"Read your lovely scriptures then, I take it." Too hard to resist.

He snorted. "This dark spirit, the one troubling your bog, it has a lair, yes?"

"Had."

The priest squinted, finishing his study of me with a nod. "Had. And now we need Pauthor to expose the new one. *He* calls to Pauthor a night, and Pauthor wants to go. Once our bait has done his work, myself along with seven swords of Ansul's True will enter whichever vile hive this spirit has chosen."

I was still juggling what was the more curious: how I could actually feel how the mausoleum was no longer *His* lair, or that there was a priest who enjoyed Gormorster Toadly. The priest's plan stabbed through my musing. "Bait! You mean for Pauthor to walk in there alone?"

The priest laid his hand on mine. "Shaman, like all who are captivated by the dark arts, you're a utilitarian. I understand. We're not so different, you and I. I am what you could call a specialist. This, don't you see, it's why I requested positions responsible for combating the forces of darkness…darkness's undeniable allure."

I was mystified.

But, sound or not, none of this syllogism meant sending Pauthor to what was certainly his doom. I recoiled my hand.

"No matter the risks," the priest went on, "this enemy has gorged on blood. Our lands can and will be harmed, but right now, at this very and most pressing moment, the warfront is your Amden Bog."

Though my mouth remained slack, my mind was busy at work. Pauthor's art adorned the very wall behind us, something the priest's clairvoyance had seemingly failed to detect. I enjoyed and respected Pauthor as an artist, and now pitied him as a man. I'd treated others as means to ends, this I could not deny, but I was no devil.

"So Pauthor is truly to be savior of the bog," I sighed.

The priest rose, stilling his pendants, nodding too proudly for the occasion. "Into the beast's belly."

"Lover of Toadly or not," I said, "you, sir, are as similar to me as a bog spring is to a clogged sewer." I'd reclaimed my cup and emptied its contents. I'd fortified my position and puffed out my chest.

I'd also gone too far.

His look was of the friend scorned. I soon reclaimed my wits. It was not the priest's fault he was in the position to be the lone messenger of sense.

Oriel's words were back. If the greatest evils came fronted as a good, then couldn't the opposite be true? Wouldn't it have to be? It was reasonable to conclude this cold and opportunistic tactic was only so at its surface level. Pauthor was not yet doomed, and though it disgusted me, Chapwyn magic had intervened, and to his favor.

From Oriel to Motty, dead men guided. "Righteous is pain," I quoted from a scroll Motty and I had seen down in that basement.

Offense that had hardened on his face began to melt. Recognizing the source, he smiled, embracing me right out of my settee. "Truly, you and I, not so different."

"You must understand," I said, getting dressed, "love for my fellow bogsmen is not something that is forced upon me by my position." He energetically agreed, handing me my sandals. "Though I often do not express it, least of all to myself." I grabbed my new staff, carved by a grateful bogling, then asked the question of the hour: "What is it exactly you want me to do?"

"My men and I will put Pauthor back in his clothes and release him. After, we trail him from a safe distance. Yes, safe. The spirit and his minions, perhaps even a familiar by now, will be able to detect our approach if we follow too closely. But you, dear Shaman, you do not smell of Chapwyn fumes. You are to follow Pauthor, serve as his clandestine protector along the way if needs be." Relieving me of my staff: "Clandestine. No weapons. The moment he reveals where the new lair is, you are to send me the location by means of a highly illegal, but highly effective telepathy spell." The priest could read my face as well as any book. "Yes, that spell. I can administer it, but only if fed to one sufficiently versed in powers manipulated and obtained outside our naïve precepts. There is no one else, nor now would I want there to be."

Vodaphul had made his way to my nightstand. Lifting another book from the pile, he said, "Did you know this was actually the first in an old trilogy?"

I winced. The book he clutched was perverted, deviant, a rally cry for nihilism. "Everyone does," I said. "Just as they know the second and third were tossed on every bonfire, sectarian and non-sectarian alike. Depravity, gruesome metaphors, so on." Toadly was one thing, but this? Yet the priest's face remained amiable.

"I own the second... and the third. Confiscated by means you may object to, yes, but I have them." He walked up close enough that I could smell olives on his breath. "Finish this dreadful task, and they're yours."

"Why?" I gaped.

"I am as you are."

Oriel had been right. And I had been also, having recognized the reverse moral in his words. Vodaphul and I shook hands.

)X(

When the Municipal One was called the Conqueror, his ambition had been simple: unite the Orisulan peninsula. Though our three great cities had always shown a mild eagerness towards trade, prior to his rather stunning success, ours was a fractured land, almost entirely ruled by the constantly scheming and double-dealing royal houses. Once under a single banner, the peninsula was renamed Rehleia, after some woman, while still soaking in the blood of men. United, yes, but with it came intrusions to people's ways the land over. His practices even came to us boglings.

I'd canoed alone to this dirt many times. It was for those nights when I couldn't sleep and no book nor bottle nor whore could provide me a lullaby. Not far from the jail grounds, the trees taller here; they loomed down together, a distant, otherworldly mountain. I'd also walked unhindered amongst the strong trunks. But not this night. Long sobered from my morning's lowness, I treaded now in a land that only grew stakes of the impaled.

Our designated plot had spilt over. Those suspected of being members in the Order and those run afoul of a clever wisher had ensured the only way I could proceed in my current route was to slink and slither under a canopy of cold, blue feet. The only positive I could muster was this forest of suspended, death-gaped bodies helped me hide from Pauthor.

I didn't care for Pauthor being used like a worm on a fat hook, but I absolutely loathed the sensation that I was the one holding the pole. Pauthor continued onward, and, dressed in the rags of a hooded swamp harvester, I followed.

Vodaphul had seized my head in both hands and loaded me with the telepathy spell. New words were dancing in my skull, like memories I held while knowing it hadn't been I who'd experienced them. With no more effort than reciting one's favorite dish, I'd shoot Vodaphul what he needed like an arrow unleashed from a mighty bow. But what then? Pauthor's head hung. He coughed. He kept himself from falling over by grabbing at the dangling legs. What healing awaited him once this was through? And would I live to see it?

We passed the backside of the Grey Heron, where crates and tossed-out food had become a festering trash heap. The distance I trailed behind would have likely alerted anyone else, but Pauthor paid no attention to my steps. He'd paid no heed to this trash heap, one that I couldn't help but stop next to and gawk at. I felt naked and alone. Those Motty-type men whose duties the heap had once been were likely benighted in pearls and gold, at that very moment hunting Pauthor, and maybe me.

He took us where I knew he would—onto the main docks, around a boarded-up fish stand, and to where Ungerfil Qell had been killed. Our direction was pointing us closer to the part of Amden where one was in danger if daring a nighttime stroll, especially if swaying and prone to stumble.

Pauthor slipped into dock alleys that I hadn't known existed. He took us past houses locked by chains, announced by way of crude signs that so-and-so was selling this-or-that because a poor drunk, suddenly rich, drank himself into the grave.

How our town had changed. I knew, as Pauthor did, those who begged for wishes at the expense of their or others' blood were bound to orbit *Him* as the sun and moon do the world. As we entered a pinch between buildings lusting to fall into the other, I ruminated on what I'd felt in the impaling grounds when misfortune beckoned I rub against a corpse that gravity had slid low. He'd been one I'd heard about, a violent man who had gotten his coins and his jewels. He'd also gotten paranoid, clubbing an innocent in broad daylight who happened to walk too close.

I saw, I felt, I knew things because I had bled into something I wasn't supposed to. Pauthor and I had accessed constellations of mind which muddied my own the more I tried to understand. Though I could not read Pauthor's thoughts, I knew why he'd wished, though not what for. As he, and the rest, must have had the same partial understanding about me. Though I was a member, my inclusion had been by way of accident, my "wish" one of absentminded folly.

To the gods—*ugh!* If I had only known, my wish would have been—I kept telling myself, trying not to feel as sanctimonious and self-adoring as I'd at first seen the priest—to get us out of this fix, not a damn *Beast Summoner*. I patted its bulge, having kept it in my satchel along with every other piece of junk that might save my hide if things went awry.

Pauthor's gait gained balance. My heart raced. We were being pulled. I had a growing suspicion—no, not exactly, more a feeling, the type which thrums outward from the bowels until demanding to be known as an infallible truth. I knew what our final destination was, revealing itself the way the forward-most shore of an approaching island is revealed through thick morning fog.

Amden's seediest dock moaned beneath me. Walls of shadow embraced, taking Pauthor in its enveloping blackness. Nature had been perverted here. I may have worried over losing sight of him if we hadn't both been getting reeled in by the same force. Just then

I emerged under the stars. The waters beyond the dock reflected a low, all-seeing moon.

When I turned to my left, I saw Pauthor standing at the hole of the lair. As I'd known, it was a decrepit little tavern.

"Motty's?" escaped my lips. I could hardly believe the sign above the door. Then it all made sense, clicking together like dungeon locks. Finding the thickest stretch of shadow, each forward placement of my sandals demanded a confidence in me that was faltering fast.

It was foolish of the priest to call me compassionate. I wanted nothing more than to abandon my errand and slam shut my eyes, only to open them from the comfort of a warm and familiar bed. In the moonlight, Pauthor was a statue carved of wood, one delivered to the door of its soon and forever-to-be owner.

Now that I knew the liar's name, I was confident I could get my brother, and more importantly his henchmen. But a vision of such men melted into one of Ansul's True. Suddenly dark shapes emerged from the night. They grabbed Pauthor, then slipped inside.

Without a staff to confirm them, my hands had ceased to feel. I expected my ears to be filled with the chaos that was to erupt inside, the lamb for the long-awaited slaughter. I heard only the wind in the trees and the slaps and calls of unstill waters.

I dithered. All strategy had been defiled by the lone advice I deprive myself of a solid weapon. I wanted to run. I wanted to hide, perhaps forever. But every fiber of my being howled Pauthor needed me, right now. Without him, we'd lose our only chance. My obligation crashed in from the roof of my mind. I fulfilled the priest's spell, then I ran—but not away.

My hood prohibited me from seeing everything, but slow, furtive turns showed I'd ran through the door, then walked, then stopped against the back of a large gathering. Whatever I'd just crossed over into was far too vast for the confines of a tavern. Or a warehouse.

Something of its insides still lingered, though twisted and queer. Helping not the cold in my gut nor the clamminess of my hands, the banalities appeared to have also been the targets of phantasmic wishing. Too big, too small, some too far apart, others too close together, the usual bar rabble—tables and stools and mugs—had all been pushed to the sides, where the air's purplish mist gave way to blackness.

The gathering, curved like a half moon, was even larger than a blood member could have known. It struck me as I tilted my gaze low and shouldered through; the Order, by the size of it, had to have pulled malcontents all the way from Oxghorde. Visions of shady pilgrims hobbling and scurrying from Pelliul and Nilghorde filled my head as I fought my trembling and waded deeper.

Pushing past murmurs and retaliatory nudges, I did my best to lay an eye on Pauthor. I was increasingly grateful for my hood, for as I neared the front, members in this assembly were being ill lit to recognition.

Though I have never been, the place sounded as I'd always imagined the sea. Torrents of noise rolled by me in an ebb and flow that disguised a whisper among angry stirs. One such latter torrent grew directly behind me. Only when I turned to see the darkened faces, eyes aflame, did I realize I'd made my way to the foremost edge.

My tremble returned. An icy lick ran up my spine, and now I wanted desperately to flee. Though I was one of them, being beyond their detection did not mean that I was beyond *His*. A bloom of flames, white and violet, spun me back around.

He loomed at the head of the gathering, before a violet fire. It gave off no smoke, was contained by no hearth, dulling or brightening with the waves of *His* hand.

He hovered in front of us. Below *Him*, centered on a tavern table, gleamed his wicked urn. *He* floated not as a shadow, but as a man. Tall and lean, *He* resembled the heathen gods I'd once admired in books of ancient, troubled lore. Every sin, every human frailty that had bled him back to form clothed him now in radiance. Smoke slithered up his legs to his face: a grim bust, keenly observant, distorted only by laughter.

Hellish howls or the bewitched bellows, I'd entered which offered no return.

Odd, but I was aware I'd lost my awareness of time. One change from *His* smirk to a worse expression could have been an hour outside. The yellow flame of his eyes, flickering from one of his subjects to another, a day. Those eyes had yet to penetrate my hood as I looked to my toes and fought off an urge to pray. My experiences with the supernatural had rendered such utterances a bad idea, especially when the supernatural is actually near. I believed then that I might experience an eternity of torment before help could arrive. Whatever fate may have been lying in wait for me was surely to be as awful as the spectacle I saw unfolding.

"Bring forth another." *He* spoke, royal, verminous, old as dust-covered bones yet blood-pumped anew. A man was dragged toward the table by wardens of the Order. For a horrid instant I thought it was Pauthor. It was only the gasps and cries and abject pleas that told me this was some other condemned soul, standing alone, shrunk to nothing against the backdrop of *His* flames.

He waved his hand.

Out from the fire walked a woman with no arms. Several children followed in a pageant of skips and struggling crawls. Their dead-white skin and missing limbs were only the beginning. "I'd told ya, ya fool of all fools, why'd ya paddle us out that way—" "Dadda!" "—Look! Look what ya did to our babies!" "Why'd you let us die out there, Father?" I am ashamed to admit it, but I was relieved when, confirming my suspicion about what had caused such ghastly amputations, crocodiles ran out to reenact their deaths, dragging the dead with them, back into the screaming flames.

The object of *His* entertainment was gifted a sudden handful of gold and then tossed back into our throng. Soon there was another, then another.

This *He* was once Moromax, a sorcerer who, from my research, had taken his corruption over the Red Isthmus in times before Amden's oldest board was a sapling. Had *His* face in those ancient days, aired those chiseled cheeks, that jaw, or were these too just manifestations of his reinstated power?

My own powers, paltry as they were, had allowed me the unbelievable: I had survived an encounter with this villain. Then, I had been stronger, for blind action in the face of genuine evil always provides a hapless fool the advantage of pure and ignorant luck. Now, to my regret, *He* had supped on the appointed lot of blood, *He* was whole, and I was no longer ignorant.

The crowd burst open. To my left, from among them, wardens pulled and kicked Pauthor forward, standing him upright. *His* moan would have sounded as if Hell itself had erupted, if it weren't for its ringing jubilation.

The Chapwyn influence still sated Pauthor, and for that alone it may have been a blessing. Pauthor looked upward, stumbling. He shivered, yes, but not as terribly as I would if chosen as the target of such horrible ire. An onlooker behind me, salivating over what Pauthor was about to receive, received the stiffness of my elbow.

I went over *His* name, daring not let it come to completeness. For surely *He* would detect me. My next move would be to charge towards the table, seize the urn, clasp Pauthor's hands about it, then together we would smash it to oblivion. But not before a little distraction. I clutched the arsenal in my pocket.

"Hide and seek now over," *He* said. Nothing constructed of flesh and blood could have rumbled such words. "Oh lowliest most important one."

"A mistake," Pauthor said. "All of it. Just let me be."

"We are sorry," rolled another dark cloud of mirth, "but those who assist in thy making are the ones who shall set you to ruin, less thwarted." Purples and shadows and us standing like fools all shifted. "The past has seen your lord, as kingdoms sprouted and crumbled, stuffed and restuffed, shapeless and senseless, back into..." The fire crackled around the urn. "Never again, Pauthor Quithot."

I took a step forward and pulled out a handful of *Lung Heavers*. Pauthor swayed.

"Besides," the awful voice moaned high above, "I don't like you." *His* habitual smile turned into a puckered kiss. "But someone used to, didn't she? And she is with us." How I heard such vileness. "Hortence issss here."

He had known I was here. Right here! This whole time. Mocking me with this taunt that he'd waited for the right moment to deliver. To hear her name, spoken on those lips.

I regained my footing and my mind, scanning the hoods and motionless heads. Had she run afoul of her worldly ambitions and come back home to fester with this brood? I would have knocked over even more of the men and women in my search, perhaps each and every one of them, if Pauthor hadn't wailed, "She's dead!" My eyes welled, not because of what his words implied, for they'd confused me. No, I gulped and glimpsed through tears as Pauthor regained himself, standing tall, valiant, crying, "She is gone! And like 'er, you and your tricks be gone!"

The flames brightened.

I was already moving. I changed my course, eyeing the urn, knocking two wardens right on their asses.

"Moroma—" but I had been leaped on. The Order aimed for my mouth, eyes, and groin. Someone pulled off my hood. "Pauthor!" I yelled, freeing my hand and hurling *Lung Heavers* through a blur of legs. "Break the urn!"

The *Heavers* had created a smoky haze that grew and grew, but had yet to blossom full. Through its wisps, *He* vanished.

"It's the shaman!" someone screamed.

The Order broke into chaos. Those in the distance drew weapons and yelled oaths. Save for those whose protracted battles with fen-lung had rendered them immune, everyone surrounding me fell to their knees. I sidestepped these scum reduced to painful wheezes. Having broken enough *Heavers* in my office to kill five men, my "immunity" came from a long-learned heuristic of accepting the pain and shallowing my breaths, both of which I applied as I made my way to Pauthor.

Pauthor was being swarmed. The hardier who stilled their lungs, and those few who'd remained unaffected, had coalesced to become a wave; one rearing back, about to crash. The urn disappeared in a bundle of snatching hands. I meant to seize Pauthor—then, if any luck was between us, carry him out like a cord of firewood.

"Get the Chapwyns!" Pauthor yelled as the wave crashed. "Get out of here, Shaman!" He needed no carrying. His lungs billowed unrestrained. In his hand, he gripped a sword.

Fights broke out all over. The last I saw of him was the sword's gleaming swirl hack down into a row of heads. The urn was no longer my priority, though I was attacked for it. I returned as best I could the punches and kicks. I ducked a flying chair to lob another salvo. The mix of *Heavers* and *Repellants* bettered my cause, pushing onward to the viscous scrum that spun and snarled where I'd last seen Pauthor. But it was a new fight which cleared my path and rallied my heart. Members attacked one another, cracking the Order in half with their obedience to *Him* and, unless my ears had lied, a renewing support for me.

With the help of a chair's leg, I got to Pauthor. He was torn, bloody, and set on high. His confiscated sword gone, he'd found another, its blade bigger, covered in blood and hair.

We fought at the other's backs. We coughed into each other's bruised and battered faces as new victims presented themselves from the ring trying to squeeze us. We began making our way to the door, and to freedom.

Particularly difficult opponents tremored when they hit the floor, releasing from their mouth's the foul shadow of their master; zipping back amongst the shadows to possess yet another. When my wild swings had reduced my weapon to splinters, I utilized moves I hadn't used since boyhood and unleashed every orb and egg of breakable magic that I'd brought for the war.

I had assumed my emotions were incapable of being pulled one way or another. I had exhausted their strings and levers to feel nothing, but now a glimmer of hope shone within the larger sensation of pure, frothing rage. However, as we pushed to the exit, once friendly faces cursed my very existence. Mad. Berserk. They lunged with their blades and swung with their clubs.

The cloud dissipating, calls for *Him* grew. A moment's search for a shaping shadow bore nothing, but the Order was rebounding, striking me with a more natural type of fear.

We had gotten within a mug's throw of the door. A final line blocked our way, but with their master nowhere to be found, they shrieked and shrunk from Pauthor's blade. The line was breaking.

Just as I was reaching for the doorknob, I felt what a rat must when a snake plunges their fangs. In my side, puncturing an organ, was a knife. The line that had blocked our way had dissolved, but it had reformed behind us. The stabber, still clinging to his knife, was a man whom I'd once given blessed fertilizer. I may have cried when I spun around fully to seize him. I put him in a headlock and fell with all my weight, feeling his neck break as we slammed into the floorboards.

Those who'd joined the offensive against us now deserted. Pauthor had relieved a final one of his arm below the elbow. From the floor, I looked up and I gasped. Unable to see it until now, in those moments I'd been unable to find Pauthor, he'd heroed forth and done the impossible. In the hand not wielding that righteous blade, Pauthor was holding the urn.

As I saw this, so did the Order. "Break it! Break it! Break it!" I shouted from the galactic distance of the tavern floor, but the voice that boomed from above drowned my desperate words.

Without the command of their leader, there had been no order—no Order. There had been no organization; a symptom of their greeds and envies. Perhaps less to their fault, most were forever limited, trying to capture two driven men added to their long list of dimness.

But now *He* had rumbled. *He'd* growled. Those who had for but a brave moment fought for us, for me, had dissolved back into the crowd. I kicked down legs and clawed and bit my way to my feet, for now they'd been called to action. And they were on us.

The blade in my hide was pulled free, but not before it had been rammed deep and twisted. "Break the fuckin' thing!" I screamed. With a wild kick, I aimed to send it into the rafters and back down in pieces. I missed, upending myself in a calamitous slide.

I must have shut my eyes to brace for impact. I shot up the moment the wind had finished fleeing my lungs. I was sitting on the dock. That sign, *Motty's*, swung directly above. The tavern was locked, and not a single light flickered behind its night-touched windows.

I sat still and I bled. Blood and snot dripped from my nose. I pressed my palm to my side where blood flowed between my fingers. Pauthor had made it too, though his sword appeared to have been lost. He lay near the dock's edge, motionless and—my heart leaped—still clutching the object of the hour. Whatever barrier we'd crossed had stopped our pursuers.

Except one.

There was every reason to believe it was over, the end of our efforts manifest in the towering shadow grown back into a man. *He* stood above Pauthor, eyeing what Pauthor held. *He* was to destroy me, my bog, then surely usher in some obscure blackness that would uproot every good me or my kind had ever bothered over. When I realized I'd staggered to my feet, I also realized one of *His* limitations persisted, perhaps always would: *He* couldn't pick up the urn.

If touching the world is to be alive, then *He* was "still hopelessly dead." I'd said it without thought, but it rang deliberate, just, and it stirred *Him* and Pauthor.

He looked not at me, but through. Those yellow slits pierced me like spears, and the result climbed up onto the dock. The light of the moon only illuminated an arm, the tossing back of her wet hair, but it was Hortence.

To the lowest pit of Hell, I could actually hear her! "Vernónn fucked me better," she cooed over and over, having crawled on top of Pauthor, holding him by the wrists to giggle into his screams. *He* had chosen the perfect weapon, easy to do when able to peer into the loves, shames, and fear of your enemies. My back pressed against the tavern wall. I gaped, still as stars, listening to Pauthor's incoherent pleas.

I will not list nor repeat what she did to Pauthor, only that when she was done, he was once again lifeless and limp. Whatever he had regained in the battle, he'd lost on the boards of the dock. *He* then pointed at me. Though her head was buried against Pauthor's, as if upon command, Hortence stood and straightened her bloody, swamp-soaked garments.

She walked towards me. It was her—my niece. She asked me to kill Pauthor, to finish it, for they couldn't. I wanted to, too. An urge had captured me. A few moments ago, I'd done to men and women things from which there was no recovery. Pauthor was just another, one in this grand blunder. And in it, this, *He* was smiling.

"Shaman," *He* hissed. "Oh, Shaman. Be my weapon."

"Weapon, yes!" I cried, detaching at last from the wall. I was familiar with certain powers, yes, and those powers had taught me. She was wrong—those unlivable lacerations and the look of glazed depravity in her eyes. Hortence wasn't real, and I confirmed this by shouldering her illusion to the dock, where it broke into a thousand pieces. "Moromax Misrael!" I cried. "Back to oblivion!"

Pauthor had risen and leaned against a dock post, where he gulped in the night air. With *His* name spoken, *He* stumbled. *His* black corpus sputtered, then turned into a thick, greasy smoke before shooting across the dock and disappearing into Pauthor.

Pauthor bent down, perhaps the man I'd known. He stood up, with the urn, leering. "Not this night, Shaman," he laughed, his eyes inhuman yellow and flickering. "No more wishes."

I did so without hope. I did so without pity or fear, but I also did so without malice. And I did not hesitate. I pulled from my satchel the *Beast Summoner*, and then I smashed it against the planks.

I would later cry unhinged for Pauthor, his dismal and unnegotiable role. What burst from the waters knocked me back and then down. A cataclysm of teeth and claws and a huge whipping tail. Beautiful—fierce beyond words, in motion, more than my imagination could have ever hoped to have mustered. The Gorsuka seized Pauthor in its jaws, swallowing every bit of him, including the urn he hugged until it broke in the sickening cacophony of crunches.

Around the time the waters regained their black tranquility, a batch of Pelat croc hunters appeared, outfitted in the blades and hides of their trade and custom. A spokesmen said, "Heard splash, Tree Wizard," the epithet their term for a Rehleian shaman. "Big big croc around?"

Up until then, I'd always regarded the Pelats with much the same snobbishness that had pelted me from the Chapwyn parapet.

Weakened and still bleeding, I was never happier in my life to be lifted by such skinny, tattooed claws.

They took me to one of their homes, where I was doctored by their heathen pastes and lathers. It was only when I marveled how they'd stopped my side from hemorrhaging that I realized Vodaphul and his men had never arrived.

X

That was soon made up for. At dawn, Ansul's True tore open the Pelat's thatched door. The Pelats were spared, but I was taken into custody and tossed in jail.

It is from here that I write.

I was brought in on the following charges: *Vandalism of a stained glass window, assistance in a prisoner's escape*, and *destruction of government property*. The evidence reweighed, I was soon charged with the murder of my faithful guard, Gax, who'd discovered my treacherous ways and was stopped by way of bludgeon before able to bravely report his findings to the commissioners. The rest, after my rabid protests that no such charges were in statute, were shoved in my face from the insides of a monstrous Chapwyn law book: *Assistance in summoning a spirit to demean or destabilize a local government, discharge of a telepathy spell*, and finally, after excited interrogations that exhausted themselves tumbling and weaving in and out of every room that held a candle, scroll, and a scribbler, after Vodaphul's slobbering interest over what happened to Pauthor was blocked by my silence: *murder by unnatural methods*. My rebuttal that such laws did not preside over the boglands only tightened my irons.

When the Order scum had unscummed themselves from wherever they'd been—or had *gone*—after Pauthor and I had spilled out of that tavern, the vilest among them who could still talk or breathe silenced their timid counterparts, allowing only an articulate few to corroborate with a priest-guided retelling of events.

Amden's support for me, I learned while lingering in my cell, remained divided. My brother, after a long and tedious petition that was rejected twice, was able to honor my request and provided me with this stack of parchment. On it this ink I spill.

The new jail sprouted up exactly where the old one had been. You can only love the bog's aggregate lack of imagination. This jail is exactly the same as its burned-down predecessor, the only distinctions being the robust and redundant fortifications. These additions, of course, are meant to prevent me from conjuring up yet another dark miracle. If I were to do so, I don't think there'd be room to include it on my charging affidavit.

I am glad my brother visits, though I am made uncomfortable by his continuous pleas I cooperate with Qell's ever-growing demands. No, the statement I shall write will be different. Emasil will come to accept this. He is the more pliable, thus the more fit for survival. It is of no consequence, but amusing nonetheless: when he visits to plea and cry and reconfirm my story for the umpteenth time, he does so standing where I stood the night I'd met Matina, and, to my best guess, I sit now in the space she'd occupied before somehow escaping a doom that I'm afraid I am unable.

I write these truths and I wait, for what I do not know. Most nights I lie awake, imagining a beach like the ones the Pelats spoke about, during my last hours as a free man. Free, that I had been, like that great creature that swallowed whole who the world will forever know as my spree's final victim. Swallowed then sank below, where I hope she still glides.

EPILOGUE

To Commissioner Murgle Qell,

Greetings from the humble chambers of Amden's first Chapwyn church! I wanted to take a moment to detach myself from the season's ceremony and indoctrinations to recap our successes and to also address some of our outstanding issues.

Our plan to guide Pauthor Quithot and Boraor Rehton (by unconventional methods) to rid the bog of its spirit problem was a stunning success. A sure sign of Tersiona's grace, our plan has worked without so much a thorn in our collective thumb.

Your justifiable ambition to modernize these lands was, as urged, you may recall, achieved by showing the people that "Chapwyn magic" is the superior. Though I do not care for the term, the sentiment is perfectly accurate.

As to your primary concern, Boraor Rehton was correctly associated and properly adjudicated for his crimes against decency and of man. Though, as all stewards of good, we are forced to be utilitarian from time to time, based on our liberal findings regarding the "shaman's" most recent involvements with the supernatural, it is with the utmost certainty I write you now that the foul man's involvement in an unknown number of past incidents more than justifies his place on a stake, which was carried out this morning before his brother could convolute our progress with an appeal, as per your esteemed guidance.

Soon the good graces of Chapwynite reach, alongside the secular but obedient iron of the Municipal One's Metropolitan Ward, will bring to your oppressively hot but not-without-its-charm bog renewed stability and unprecedented prosperity, sparing (obviously) that which was a result of black magic.

I feel it is worth mentioning, my men found a number of hidden books in Boraor's home. The contents of these literary maladies only prove all the more the man's less than admirable sensibilities. For safekeeping, the books have been put in the trust of yours truly.

On a closing, yet oddly related note, I've confiscated his deeply untrustworthy but highly entertaining entries that were left in his jail cell. I must concede a shameful but harm-less interest in writing fiction. That noted, I'll be taking the liberty of using the fruits of our interrogations and the boorish but ample bog lore to, as some writers say, "Fill in the gaps." Once completed, the collection will be submitted to the very best Oxghorde publishers for distribution. Purely fictional. Further discussions as to royalties, profit sharing, and the like shall to be set at our mutual convenience.

You had done right to send for ~~my~~ Chapwyn assistance when matters escalated down here. Ridding the world of its abominable dangers takes a great deal of time, effort, and especially money. I feel there is still much work to be done. Even now, your waters nearest my pulpit window stir with the shimmer and roll of a living, fearful discontent. As if stirred by an evil and mighty tail.

Sincerely and truest yours; Priest Vodaphul, High Priest Select